THIS WALKER BOOK BELONGS TO:

FOR EVERY KID ON THE PLANET – YOU DESERVE TO BE THE BOSS. AND WITH THANKS TO OISIN, ST MACARTAN'S AND ALL THE OTHER KIDS IN DONEGAL FOR THEIR HELP. – L.H.

TO BILLIE, MADELEINE ET CIBOULETTE. – J.D.

First published 2025 by Walker Books Ltd
87 Vauxhall Walk, London SE11 5HJ

2 4 6 8 10 9 7 5 3 1

EU Authorized Representative: HackettFlynn Ltd, 36 Cloch Choirneal, Balrothery, Co. Dublin, K32 C942, Ireland. EU@walkerpublishinggroup.com

This book has been typeset in Futura, Academy Engraved, Annie Use Your Telescope, Autumn Voyage, Display Patrol, Fat Free Solid, Likely, Liquid Embrace, Malayalam Sangam, Marker Monkey, Minion, Ribeye, Travelling Typewriter and Wingdings

Printed and bound by CPI Group (UK) Ltd, Croydon, CR0 4YY

British Library Cataloguing in Publication Data:
a catalogue record for this book is available from the British Library

ISBN 978-1-5295-0664-8

www.walker.co.uk

All activities are for information and/or entertainment purposes only.
Adult supervision is required for all activities.

WALKER BOOKS

FSC
www.fsc.org
MIX
Paper | Supporting responsible forestry
FSC® C013604

HOW TO OUTSMART A GROWN-UP

LARRY HAYES

ILLUSTRATED BY JOËLLE DREIDEMY

CONTENTS

SECRET NUMBER 1

HOW TO DO A JEDI MIND TRICK

EVERYBODY THINKS:

Jedi mind tricks are pure fantasy. All that "mind touch" nonsense is totally made up. It's impossible to control another person's brain just by waving your hand and talking in a soft voice.

BUT SECRET 1 IS THIS:

It is possible to influence what other people do and think using a few psychological techniques inspired by the Star Wars movies.
We've already revealed how to get Jedi mind powers in *How to Be a Kid Boss:* you really need to buy it if you want to be happy. But now it's time to learn how to channel you inner Jedi to get what you want.

PUT IT TO THE TEST:

JEDI MIND TRICKS:

TRICK 1: ELBOW TOUCH

Briefly touch somebody at the top of the elbow just before asking for something – and they usually say yes.

TRICK 2: FOOT IN THE DOOR

Ask for a *small* favour first, something really easy for them to do. Then ask for a bigger favour within a few minutes and they'll be much more likely to agree.

TRICK 3: GO BIG THEN GO SMALL

The reverse of the above is even more powerful. Ask for a *big* favour. When they refuse, ask for what you really want.

TRICK 4: SHOW YOUR PALMS

It makes you more believable.

THE NEXT TRICK is so good, it needs its own Secret. This Jedi mind trick is the most fun you can humanly have at school. It's called **Secret 2: How to mind-control your teacher.**

> Why are you still reading this page? Go to **Secret 2: How to mind-control your teacher**.

SECRET NUMBER 2

HOW TO MIND-CONTROL YOUR TEACHER

EVERYBODY THINKS:

Teachers are in charge. Children must obey. School is a place of work and effort and doing what you're told.

BUT SECRET 2 IS THIS:

You can mind-control your teacher with a Jedi mind trick.[1] First, you need to learn a simple thing about human brains: we like attention. And even teachers are human. Here is a step-by-step guide to mind-control your teacher:

STEP 1: ASK FRIENDS TO HELP

Get them to read this page.

STEP 2: ALL CHOOSE ONE CORNER OF THE CLASSROOM

You are going to get your teacher to stand in that corner.

STEP 3: WHEN YOUR TEACHER GETS CLOSER TO THE CORNER

Pay extra attention to the lesson – everyone needs to look more interested.

STEP 4: IF THEY MOVE AWAY FROM THE CORNER

Look less interested in what they're saying.

STEP 5: WITHOUT EVEN REALIZING WHY

Your teacher will gradually find themselves moving closer and closer to the corner.

PUT IT TO THE TEST:

Go on, we double dare you.

---

[1] For others, see **Secret 1: How to do a Jedi mind trick**.

HOW TO TELL WHEN A GROWN-UP'S LYING

EVERYBODY THINKS:

Lying is bad.

BUT SECRET 3 IS THIS:

Everybody lies. Well, apart from babies. Most people learn to lie by about 3 years old. Lies come in two flavours: prosocial and antisocial.

PROSOCIAL LIES = told for someone *else's* benefit.
ANTISOCIAL LIES = told strictly for your own personal gain.

Most grown-up lies are *prosocial* – they're trying to be kind, so don't be too hard on them. But sometimes grown-ups lie for an easier life.

PUT IT TO THE TEST:

Here are the "Big Five" grown-up lies. Recognize any?

WHAT THEY SAY	vs	WHAT THEY MEAN
☐ YES, WE'RE NEARLY THERE.		☐ PLEASE STOP MOANING.
☐ FATHER CHRISTMAS KEEPS A NAUGHTY LIST.		☐ PLEASE STOP BEING NAUGHTY.
☐ EATING CARROTS WILL HELP YOU SEE IN THE DARK.		☐ PLEASE EAT A VEGETABLE FOR ONCE IN YOUR LIFE!
☐ IF THE WIND CHANGES YOUR FACE WILL STAY LIKE THAT.		☐ THAT FACE IS CREEPING ME OUT.
☐ THAT DRAWING IS BEAUTIFUL!		☐ WE LOVE YOU, EVEN IF YOUR DRAWING IS RUBBISH.

SECRET NUMBER 4

HOW TO TELL WHAT SOMEONE IS REALLY THINKING

EVERYBODY THINKS:

Psychologists are terrifying because they can often tell exactly what you're thinking just by reading your body language. If you point your foot in a certain direction or look to the left when you're talking, they will *know everything that's going on in your head.* But it takes years to become a psychologist and the rest of us have no way of knowing what other people are thinking.

BUT SECRET 4 IS THIS:

With a few psychology tips and a bit of practice, you too can become a pro body-language reader.

1. Raised eyebrows often signal discomfort.
2. If their voice goes up or down in pitch, they're probably interested in what you're saying. Eye contact shows they're interested… But if they look into your eyes for too long, they might be lying.
3. Crossed legs or arms are usually a sign of resistance or low interest.
4. If they "mirror" your body language, they like you.
5. Crinkles around the eyes show they're smiling for real.
6. If they're laughing with you, they probably like you.
7. Watch out for "micro expressions" – small and quick smiles, frowns or grimaces that slip out.

WARNING! These don't *always* work. They work best when you know what the person is normally like. For example, if someone is *always* fidgeting they're probably not bored, they're just being their usual fidgety self.

HOW TO READ BODY LANGUAGE

PUT IT TO THE TEST:

The best way to practise is by playing "Two Truths and a Lie" to fast-track your psychology super-skills.

PLAY TWO TRUTHS AND A LIE

Each person says two truths and one lie about themselves. The others have to guess which is the lie...

SECRET NUMBER 5

HOW TO CHEAT A LIE DETECTOR

EVERYBODY THINKS:

You can't cheat a lie detector – they're all sciencey and clever.

BUT SECRET 5 IS THIS:

Cheating a lie detector is actually really easy.[2] But first, you need to understand how a lie detector works. A typical lie detector measures three things. All of these go up or get faster when you lie because you're a bit nervous:

1. **HEART RATE AND BLOOD PRESSURE**
2. **BREATHING**
3. **SKIN SWEAT**

But to measure if something changes, they first need to know what your *normal* level is. They test normal levels by asking you "control" questions where they know you're telling the truth. The control questions tell the machine what your normal levels are. Let's take a look at a typical lie detector investigation:

HOW A LIE DETECTOR WORKS:

[2] Or is it? We might be lying…

Now here's where the cheat comes in. You need to make yourself feel worried *when you answer the control question*. That way, the detector won't measure any difference when you lie. Just imagine you're being chased by a zombie or a standing on the edge of a cliff. Whatever makes you most scared in life.

HOW TO CHEAT A LIE DETECTOR:

PUT IT TO THE TEST:

If you can, download a lie detector app onto a phone or computer and start thinking about zombies. (Please do this before reading **Secret 74: How to survive a zombie apocalypse**. Once you've read that, zombies won't seem scary any more.) If it doesn't work, please write to us and we'll send you eight million pounds (no word of a lie).[3]

[3] Note from the publishers: this is definitely a lie.

SECRET NUMBER 6

HOW TO WIN ANY ARGUMENT

EVERYBODY THINKS:

The winner of an argument is the person who is right.

BUT SECRET 6 IS THIS:

Nope, if that were the case then we'd always have the best leaders, no one would go to jail for a crime they didn't commit and life would be fair. Sadly, none of these things are true. The winner of any argument is usually the person who is best at arguing. Here's five top tips for making a better argument:

TIP 1: STAY CALM

This can be easier said than done. Try a "Magic Double Breath" to instantly calm yourself down (for full details see **Secret 25: How to not blush**).

TIP 2: ASK HOW

We're more stupid than we think. So, asking people to explain things in detail will quickly show them what they don't know. Asking them "how" things work is really effective.

TIP 3: GIVE THEM KNOWLEDGE

Give them some facts. Just make sure you've done your homework.

TIP 4: DIFFERENT PERSPECTIVE

Ask them what they would think if they were someone else.

TIP 5: BE KIND

Treat them nicely and don't rub it in with an "I told you so".

PUT IT TO THE TEST:

Let's look at one common area of argument: *bedtime.*

HOW TO WIN AN ARGUMENT ABOUT BEDTIME:

SECRET NUMBER 7

HOW TO MAKE EVERYONE SHUT UP AND LISTEN (FOR ONCE)

EVERYBODY THINKS:

Children should be seen and not heard. After all, you're just a kid – what do you know? And it's not just adults who think that. Older siblings are *the worst*. They think they have the right to talk over anyone younger than them. Does this sound familiar?

BUT SECRET 7 IS THIS:

What you have to say is often important. Children have just as much right to be heard as anyone else. Making yourself heard, whether in an argument or in a group project at school, is a vital skill.

So, if you ever feel like you're speaking with the mute button on, try these six tips for getting people to listen.

MAKE YOURSELF HEARD, SIX TOP TIPS:

TIP 1: LOCATION, LOCATION, LOCATION Where you sit matters. In a group, sit as close to the centre of the table as possible. If you need to, be prepared to stand up to make your point.

TIP 2: QUESTIONS NOT ANSWERS Starting with a question can make everyone stop and pause. Then be ready to answer your own question.

TIP 3: HEADLINE FIRST Cut the back story – get straight to the main point.

TIP 4: I NOT YOU If you start a sentence with "you" people often go into defensive mode and stop listening. Express vulnerability rather than anger by starting sentences with "I".

TIP 5: CALL THEM OUT If someone talks over you, point it out with an assertive "Can I please finish my point?"

TIP 6: BE SUPER PREPARED Have the info ready to support your argument. (Also read **Secret 6: How to win any argument**.)

PUT IT TO THE TEST:

Spot the difference between these two conversations. Can you spot all six tips in action in the "DO THIS" picture?

SECRET NUMBER 8

HOW TO BECOME THE WORLD'S GREATEST FOOTBALLER

EVERYBODY THINKS:

The world's greatest footballers are born that way. Unless you're destined to be tall, strong, fast, agile, fearless and with two right feet – you don't have a hope.

BUT SECRET 8 IS THIS:

The greatest footballers of all time come in all shapes and sizes. Arguably the two greatest of all time, Lionel Messi and Marta Vieira da Silva, are both shorter than an average footballer's height. What they have in common are five key abilities, and you can train all of them.

1. DRIBBLING SPEED

Both Marta and Messi can almost run as fast *with* the ball as without it. They both lose only a small percentage of their speed.

2. FOOTBALL IQ

When scientists tested Marta's peripheral vision it was off the charts. Messi's passing and vision on the field made him not only the top goal scorer, but also the player with the most "assists".

3. SKILL WITH BOTH FEET

Marta scored her greatest ever World Cup goal with her "weaker" right foot. Messi could also score goals with his left or right foot.

4. AGILITY

Marta's signature move was dancing past defenders. Messi could zigzag through cones faster than an Olympic sprinter.

5. DURABILITY

Marta played in a record, 6 World Cups, spanning 16 years. Messi missed very few games a year through injury over his 13 years at the top.

PUT IT TO THE TEST:

How many times have you heard the phrase "Practise, practise, practise." You may have heard about the "10,000 Hour Rule" too. You need to practise something for 10,000 hours to become a true master. Well, to hit 10,000 hours by the time you're 18 years old means spending an hour and a half a day practising football.

But what should you do during those 90 minutes a day?

WORLD'S GREATEST FOOTBALLER TRAINING PLAN

PLAY THE WALL

Super skill your passing and first touch by kicking the ball against a wall. Switch from left to right foot. Search online for "Wall drills" for ideas and challenges.

DRIBBLE

Run on the balls of your feet using the front/outside of your boot to kick the ball. Get someone to clock your speeds over 20 metres.

GO THE EXTRA 10

The world's best players are usually the last off the training pitch. Spend 10 minutes at the end of every training session practising with your weaker foot – shots and crosses. Give yourself a target and go for it.

PLAY ALL POSITIONS

Play all 11 positions on the pitch. This is the number one way to boost your football IQ, develop your tactical awareness and understand how the game is played from all angles.

TRAMPOLINE

20 minutes a day will build your leg strength for speed, stamina and strength. Helping you stay injury-free.

SHUTTLE RUNS

For strength, speed and agility nothing beats shuttle runs. Run between two points 10 metres apart, touching the ground before you switch. Time yourself for 100 metres to track your improvement.

SECRET NUMBER 9

HOW TO SAVE A PENALTY

EVERYBODY THINKS:

Saving penalties is all down to luck: it's a fifty–fifty chance you'll dive the right way.

BUT SECRET 9 IS THIS:

Scientists have studied this too, because saving penalties is BIG business. There are three main areas to focus on: your technique, where they're going to shoot and mind tricks. Having trawled all the research we can now, finally, share the secret of the Ultimate Guide to Saving a Penalty.

ULTIMATE GUIDE TO SAVING A PENALTY

GET IN THEIR HEAD
Tell them you know where they're going to shoot.

WATCH THEIR EYES
They'll look where they want to shoot.

FEET
Watch their "plant foot" it will point in the direction they're going to shoot. So if you choose to dive, dive that way.

SECRET NUMBER 10

HOW TO DRAW SOMETHING AMAZING

EVERYBODY THINKS:

Artists are born arty. Or maybe they have to practise loads. I dunno, I'm a writer. But either way, if you can't draw, you can't draw.

BUT SECRET 10 IS THIS:

Anyone can draw. Better still, with a couple of tricks, anyone can draw something amazing. Yeah, sure, you have to practise loads to be really good at everything like Joëlle, but with a little help even Larry Hayes could draw *one* really cool cartoon. Over to you, Joëlle:

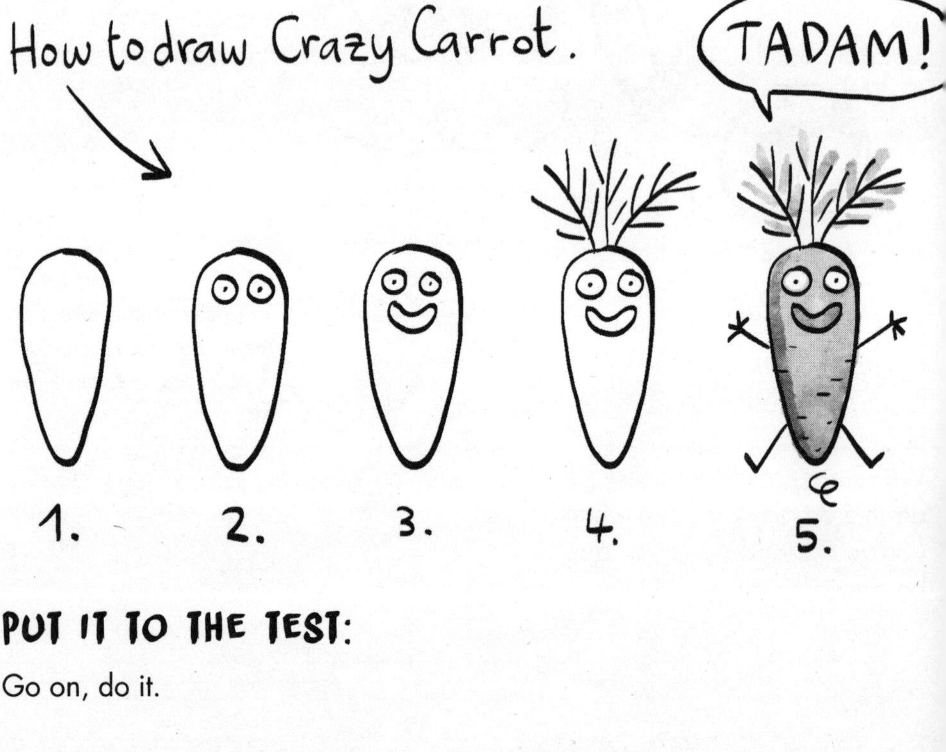

PUT IT TO THE TEST:

Go on, do it.

HOW TO MAKE A FRIEND FOR LIFE

EVERYBODY THINKS:

Some friendships last for ever and some don't. There's nothing you can do about it. With time your interests, activities and plans for the future change and the same is true for your friends. Just because you liked My Little Pony or fart jokes when you were 5, it doesn't mean you'll like the same things when you're 25. Whether you stay friends is all down to dumb luck.

BUT SECRET 11 IS THIS:

According to psychologists, friendships that last more than seven years are more likely than not to last a lifetime. You may not see them all the time, but catching up with old friends is often comforting and free from misunderstanding because you have a shared history. They already know how weird you are, and vice versa.

PUT IT TO THE TEST:

There's only one key thing to making a friend for life: you need to both let your guard down and talk about your fears, flaws, mistakes, hopes and worries.
We're not saying you should do this on day one: But when you've a friend you trust, don't be afraid to share.

SECRET NUMBER 12

HOW TO TURN AN ENEMY INTO A FRIEND

EVERYBODY THINKS:

Once a deadly enemy, always a deadly enemy. The best you can hope for to avoid them. And that's not easy when you go to the same school.

BUT SECRET 12 IS THIS:

Learning that someone hates you can be one of the most alarming things we face in life, but try not to panic. You *can* make things better and even turn things around completely. But first, you need to learn a little psychology.

THE PSYCHOLOGY OF ENEMIES

DON'T PANIC: You're not alone. Every decent and interesting person is going to have enemies at some point. Remember, the bullying isn't about you. The problem is always with the person who bullies.

FIND OUT WHY: Maybe they're jealous of you, or afraid of you. Often, it's based on a misunderstanding, or because they think *you* don't like *them*.

DIAL IT DOWN: Minimize the problem by avoiding and ignoring them as much as possible. When you have to interact, keep it short, sweet and respectful. Resist the temptation to bully them back. But do try to stand up for yourself, and call them out when they're behaving badly.

TELL SOMEONE: Whether that be a teacher, parent or friend, let others know about the situation. These figures can help intervene and advocate for you or the person being bullied and let them reassure you that you don't deserve the hate.

BUT WHAT ABOUT TURNING AN ENEMY INTO A FRIEND? Surely that's impossible? Well, no. There's one clever trick for doing just that: asking them for help. It will send the message that you value them. And it will be incredibly hard for them to stay mean.

WARNING! Even if you use these psychology tips, it doesn't mean that an enemy will want to be friends. But try not to worry, give them space and put your energy into the friends you do have.

PUT IT TO THE TEST:

HOW TO ASK YOUR DEADLY ENEMY FOR HELP:

SECRET NUMBER 13

HOW TO STOP BITING YOUR NAILS

EVERYBODY THINKS:

It's impossible to stop biting your nails. Most people bite their nails when they're bored or worried. So, once you get into the habit, you're stuck biting them for life.

BUT SECRET 13 IS THIS:

You *can* stop biting nails – millions of people stop every year. But most people try the wrong things.

WHAT DOESN'T WORK:

WILLPOWER
Your willpower will get exhausted after a few days or you'll forget and do it absent-mindedly.

WEARING MITTENS ALL THE TIME
Not practical.

BEING SHOUTED AT
Doesn't help, just makes you feel worse.

THINKING ABOUT ALL THE GERMS ON YOUR HAND
This will just make you even more stressed out.

What does work, based on our experiments on small children, are two things. You just need strong motivation, and something really disgusting.

PUT IT TO THE TEST:

WHAT WILL WORK:

THING 1: MOTIVATION If it's your parent or carer who wants you stop … then you need some added motivation. Tell them this.

THING 2: BITTER NAIL PAINT Designed to stop you biting your nails. The good stuff lasts *two whole days*.

HOW TO LICK THE OUTSIDE OF YOUR ELBOW

EVERYBODY THINKS:

No one can lick the outside of their elbow. And if you try, you end up looking stupid.

BUT SECRET 14 IS THIS:

That's just not true. About 1% of the population can do it, usually for one of two reasons:

REASON 1: THEY HAVE REALLY LONG TONGUES

- The world record is 10.1cm (measured from the place in the back of the throat where the tongue begins to the tip).
- The average tongue is 7.9cm (women) and 8.5cm (men).
- The average 10 year old's is 6.7cm.

REASON 2: HYPERMOBILITY

Where people have really flexible joints (neck, shoulder and elbow are important for this challenge).

PUT IT TO THE TEST:

Try to lick the outside of your elbow. Are you one of the 1% who can do it? This is the best technique:

1. Go for your left elbow if you're right-handed because your weaker shoulder should be more flexible (so use the right elbow if you're left-handed).
2. Pull your arm into your neck with your other hand.
3. Push you bottom jaw forward to free up your tongue to lick over the top of your arm.
4. Expect to look weird while you're doing it.

WARNING! If it starts to hurt or if you hear any cracking or popping sounds, STOP. It's not worth it.

SECRET NUMBER 15

HOW TO STOP A FART (FOR A BIT)

EVERYBODY THINKS:

Everybody farts and there's no stopping it. Once the pressure builds, something's gotta give. If it doesn't come out the bottom end, it'll have to come out the other end, at the top. And no one wants that.

BUT SECRET 15 IS THIS:

There are times in life when it's really useful to stop a fart. Secret agents, ninjas and even teachers[4] are trained to make sure they only fart when it's safe to do so. A fart at the wrong time could end a teacher's career. Especially if you're called Mr Pants.

FOR THE REST OF HIS CAREER, HE WAS KNOWN TO GENERATIONS OF SCHOOLCHILDREN AS MR FARTYPANTS.

---

[4] Probably.

PUT IT TO THE TEST:

HOW TO HOLD IN A FART SAFELY:

TIP 1: DON'T HOLD IT IN FOR TOO LONG.

TIP 2: CLENCH YOUR BUTTOCKS LIKE YOUR LIFE DEPENDS ON IT.

TIP 3: LEAN FORWARD TO EASE THE PRESSURE.

TIP 4: STAND UP STRAIGHT TO GIVE YOUR FART MORE ROOM.

IF IT FAILS:

RELEASE THE FART SLOWLY: If you're in public and have no escape route and know that the fart is coming any second now, then your best bet is to slowly release it. Slowly unclench your butt cheeks, wiggle around a bit to move your cheeks apart and then let the fart slowly escape from your body.

BLAME IT ON SOMEONE ELSE: See *How to Be a Kid Boss*: **Secret 51: How to blame your fart on someone else** for more tips.

ALTERNATIVELY, JUST OWN IT: It's hard to make fun of someone who's not embarrassed. Own up to the fart and name yourself tooting champion.

SECRET NUMBER 16

HOW TO NOT LAUGH WHEN SOMEONE FARTS

EVERYBODY THINKS:

It's impossible to not laugh when someone farts.

BUT SECRET 16 IS THIS:

You can hold in your chuckles with a simple trick that triggers the phrenic nerve and calms your diaphragm – the big sheet of muscle in your chest used for breathing and *laughing*. This trick is so powerful it will also guarantee you always win the "First One to Laugh" game.

We call it the Magic Double Breath.

PUT IT TO THE TEST:

THE MAGIC DOUBLE BREATH

STEP 1: Breathe in deeply through your nose…

STEP 2: Before you breath out … breathe in again! But just a short, sharp second breath in.

STEP 3: Breathe out slowly.

BONUS FACTS: This can also help calm you down when you're stressed or anxious. It can even help lower your blood pressure. A "triple breath" is generally recognized in the scientific community as the best way to get rid of hiccups[5] and, it helps you live longer.[6]

---

[5] See *How to Be a Kid Boss,* **Secret 98: How to get rid of hiccups**.

[6] See also **Secret 78: How to come back from the dead**.

HOW TO STOP PINS AND NEEDLES (FAST)

EVERYBODY THINKS:

When you get pins and needles, there's nothing you can do to get rid of them fast. You just have to wait it out while an agonizing army of (metaphorical) fire ants crawl up and down your leg or arm or whatever.

BUT SECRET 17 IS THIS:

There's a quick cure for pins and needles *wherever you get them.* But first, you need to understand what causes them.

WHAT CAUSES PINS AND NEEDLES?

PUT IT TO THE TEST:

Once you take the pressure off, the nerves get better. You can try:

1. Turning your head slowly from side to side to loosen up the nerves in your neck.
2. Clenching and unclenching your fists to get the blood flowing.
3. Lying down and raising your feet above your heart. Then wiggle your toes to get the blood flowing.

WARNING! If you keep getting pins and needles or they don't go away, see your doctor.

SECRET NUMBER 18

HOW TO BUY A HOUSE (WHEN YOU'RE STILL A KID)

EVERYBODY THINKS:

It would be great to buy a property when you're a kid, because property just goes up and up in value so by the time you get to be an adult you'll be minted.

But everybody also thinks – you *can't* buy a house when you're just a kid, it's illegal for anyone under the age of 18 to own property. And besides, where would you get the money from?

BUT SECRET 18 IS THIS:

A child can't own property, but they can own shares in a *company* which owns a property. They just need to be 16 years old to become a company director. The trouble is, to buy even the cheapest properties in the UK, you'll need to spend a huge chunk of dosh, about £40,000. And the average property is worth seven times that! The good news is that you can get a bank loan (a mortgage) to cover most of the cost, rent out the property and use your rent to pay off the loan. The bad news is you need some money up front, called the "deposit". Buying a property can seem like a scary, complicated thing to do – even for adults. But the hardest bit is saving the deposit.

PUT IT TO THE TEST:

HOW TO SAVE UP FOR A HOUSE DEPOSIT (WHEN YOU'RE STILL A KID)

STEP 1: SET YOURSELF A TARGET

£10,000 is probably the minimum. That's a lot – but it's not impossible. Remember, you've got until your 16th birthday. Time is on your side.

STEP 2: GET SOME START UP MONEY

For all the best ideas check out **Secret 51: How to make money when you're still at school.** Give yourself an initial target of £1,000. Remember, once you've got some money behind you, you can start putting it to work!

STEP 3: PUT YOUR MONEY TO WORK

This is where the magic happens. The plan is simple: buy gadgets and then rent them out. Online rental sites let you rent out everything from campervans to sewing machines, but small gadgets work best because you can post them easily. Typically you'll cover the cost of the gadget after twenty days. So every year you can easily double your money. As long as you keep buying more gadgets to rent out… you can keep doubling your money:

Year 7: Earn £1,000 and buy some gadgets	£1,000
Year 8: Double it!	£2,000
Year 9: Double it!	£4,000
Year 10: Double it!	£8,000
Year 11: Double it![7]	£16,000

STEP 4: WAIT FOR YOUR 16TH BIRTHDAY

You'll be all set. £10,000 for a deposit plus £6,000 to spend on really, really cool trainers…

CHEAT METHOD: see **Secret 32: How to cheat at Monopoly.**

---

[7] If you keep going until you're 32, you'll be one of the world's youngest billionaires. But you'll also need a warehouse and thousands of employees.

SECRET NUMBER 19

HOW TO SAY SORRY

EVERYBODY THINKS:

Sorry is the hardest word to say. Even harder than "mischievous" and "anemone". Because if you say sorry, then you're admitting it was all your fault and you'll be blamed for everything from now on.

BUT SECRET 19 IS THIS:

Saying sorry is important – and being able to do it well will make your life easier and happier.

If you want to restore peace in your life and keep friendships happy and strong[8] learn how to say sorry.

HOW TO SAY SORRY

[8] See also **Secret 11: How to make a friend for life.**

DO APOLOGIZE (ONLY) FOR WHAT YOU DID WRONG:
I SHOULD HAVE CHECKED BEFORE EATING IT.
DON'T SAY:
I'M THE WORST SISTER IN THE WORLD!
DO MEAN IT:
I REALLY AM SORRY, THAT MUST BE AWFUL.
DON'T SAY:
SORRY, GEEZ. I DIDN'T KNOW IT WAS GOING TO BE SUCH A BIG DEAL.
DO MAKE AMENDS:
I CAN BUY YOU A REPLACEMENT USING MY POCKET MONEY.
DON'T SAY:
THERE'S ALWAYS NEXT EASTER!

HOW TO SURVIVE SWALLOWING BUBBLEGUM

EVERYBODY THINKS:

When you swallow a piece of gum it stays in your stomach for 7 years.

BUT SECRET 20 IS THIS:

It's true your body can't digest swallowed gum, but if you accidentally swallow a piece of gum, it doesn't get stuck in your stomach. It passes through into your poop. The interesting question, though, is how long does it take?

> **WARNING!** DO NOT SWALLOW GUM. On rare occasions, large amounts of swallowed gum combined with constipation has caused blocked intestines, which is obviously really dangerous. So avoid swallowing gum altogether.

The time from swallowing food to pooing it out is known as **TRANSIT TIME** and it varies from person to person. How long it takes you to poo after eating can tell you a lot about your gut, and overall health. Generally, the quicker it is, the more variety of gut bacteria you have.

A HIGH VARIETY OF GUT BACTERIA CAN HELP YOU BE:

STRONGER, FASTER, LEANER, HEALTHIER AND CLEVERER.

So why not check yours?

PUT IT TO THE TEST:

TEST YOUR TRANSIT TIME

1. EAT SWEETCORN AND START THE CLOCK – SWEETCORN IS FAMOUS FOR PASSING THROUGH YOUR BODY INTACT.

2. WAIT AND WATCH.

3. HOW LONG DID IT TAKE? CHECK YOUR RESULTS.

LESS THAN 24 HOURS = YAY, YOU'RE IN THE IDEAL RANGE.

24–48 HOURS = YOUR GUT BACTERIA NEED A BOOST: TRY EATING A WIDER RANGE OF FRUIT, VEGETABLES AND BEANS.

48 HOURS + = WOW, YOU REALLY NEED SOME FIBRE.

BONUS KNOW-HOW: It's impossible to swallow bubblegum and then fart a bubble so please don't try. By the time the gum gets to your bum, it will have lost its stickiness because of your digestive juices.

SECRET NUMBER 21

HOW TO BUY HAPPINESS

EVERYBODY THINKS:

Money can't buy happiness. There's even a saying about it that goes something like this...

BUT SECRET 21 IS:

Money can bring you happiness, but probably not how you think. It's time you learned the *truth* about spending and happiness. It all comes down to a brain chemical called dopamine.

THE TRUTH ABOUT SPENDING AND HAPPINESS

THE DOPAMINE BUZZ: When you buy stuff, your brain releases a feel-good chemical called dopamine. It's the same chemical that's released when people check their social media. And it makes you feel good.

THE BIG TROUBLE WITH DOPAMINE: It's a short-term happiness chemical. It's the "Quick Fix Happy Hormone" and it's designed (evolved) to disappear quickly. And so, attempting to always maximize dopamine, actually ends in lower long-term happiness.

HOW LONG DOES THE DOPAMINE BUZZ LAST?

If you buy say, your favourite food, the dopamine lasts about 10 minutes. Then it's gone. Even if you buy something major like a car, the dopamine buzz will only last for a few minutes a day for a month or two.

So, if you want to be happy, stop spending money. Instead, spend time: with family or friends, exercising or playing outdoors, and creating things that you love (see *How to Be a Kid Boss,* **Secret 48: How to be happy**.)

BUT HOLD ON, YOU SAID MONEY CAN BRING YOU HAPPINESS.

Yes, having enough money can bring you happiness in two ways:

HOW MONEY CAN MAKE YOU HAPPIER

LESS STRESS: Money can shield you from the shocks, crises and the anxieties of life.

MORE FREEDOM: This is the big one. As an adult, financial freedom can let you focus on pursuing a career you love, or quit a job you hate.

PUT IT TO THE TEST:

You just need to become the sort of person who attracts *and then keeps* lots of money. See **Secret 51: How to make money when you're still at school**.

WARNING! Remember, money isn't everything, so make sure you spend your time on things that will make you happy! See **Secret 44: How to dress yourself happy** and **Secret 46: How to make yourself happier with a pencil**.

HOW TO INVENT AN EPIC GAME

EVERYBODY THINKS:

It's impossible for a kid to invent a game, because it's too hard.

BUT SECRET 22 IS THIS:

Sure, video games are hard to invent and they need millions of pounds of investments. But *card games* are much easier. And the industry is booming. So, if you enjoy Dobble™ or UNO™, then why not give inventing card games a crack?

WHERE TO START

1. PLAY: Try a whole bunch of games to see what's out there. You'll get ideas about what you like, dislike and what's new and popular.

2. RULES: This is the tricky part. See what types of game you like, and then come up with a novel twist. Or maybe combine bits of two different games to come up with something new. The best games are simple to explain but allow for some cunning tactics.

3. STORY, DESIGN AND LOGO: Go for something that really stands out.

4. TEST IT! Play it with friends and (if you can) find people who play lots of games and get their opinions.

5. LAUNCH IT! Use a crowdfunding site for a zero cost, risk-free launch. Make sure a trusted grown-up helps you set this up.

PUT IT TO THE TEST:

We put this to the test, so you can see how it worked for us. We came up with:

TRUE OR GNU POO™ A MIND-BLOWING QUIZ GAME FOR THE WHOLE FAMILY

"True or Gnu Poo?"

Baby giraffes use their butts as pillows.

Yoda's last words were, "Dying I am."

Most people dream in black and white.

1. PLAY: We tried some existing quiz card games, but found it was hard to play as a family, because (sometimes) adults know a lot more stuff than kids. So, we came up with a true or false quiz game where kids have an equal chance of winning. Plus, you learn some mind-blowing facts.

2. RULES: We love quiz games but also love the "special cards" in UNO™ because they allow sneaky tactics. So, we added in some "Power Up Cards" of our own.

3. STORY, DESIGN AND LOGO: "True or False" sounds boring, so we went with "True or Gnu Poo" which has a whole backstory and gross characters.

4. TEST: When we tested this, we realized we needed facts that were truly mind-blowing.

5. LAUNCH: We're printing prototype packs ready for play-testers.

SECRET NUMBER 23

HOW TO NOT CRY

EVERYBODY THINKS:

It's OK to cry. Crying is a natural human response to joy, stress or sadness. It's healthy and natural.

BUT SECRET 23 IS THIS:

That's all true. But you still might find yourself in a situation where you *don't* want to cry, for whatever reason. If that happens then don't worry, doctors have discovered two simple tricks for stopping tears in their tracks.

1. **TONGUE PRESS:** push your tongue to the roof of your mouth.
2. **SUPER-PINCH:** pinch the skin between your thumb and pointer.

PUT IT TO THE TEST:

Watch one of these sad movies and try both tricks to see which works best for you. Here are my top four sad films – we cried just thinking about them:

#4. THE IRON GIANT This film will melt your steely heart.

#3. CHARLOTTE'S WEB We cried (and we normally hate spiders).

#2. ET There's this bit at the end … if you know, you know.

#1. UP! The top spot goes to the beginning of *Up*!

If none of these work, see **Secret 24: How to cry whenever you want**.

HOW TO CRY WHENEVER YOU WANT

EVERYBODY THINKS:

Only brilliant actors can cry whenever they want. The rest of us have to chop an onion.

BUT SECRET 24 IS THIS:

RADA, a top drama school, can teach their students how to cry in a single lesson. It takes just two things: physical triggers and a little imagination. And if that doesn't work, you can always cheat.

Remember, crying is a really important safety valve, because keeping difficult feelings inside can be bad for our physical and mental health. Crying encourages support from friends and family and flushes stress hormones out of your system.

PUT IT TO THE TEST:

IMAGINE:

A sad or heart-breaking scene in your mind. It could be from a movie, book, dream or reality. Create a vivid mental image, paying attention to the details and emotions. Engage all your senses: not just sight – but hearing, smell, taste and touch too.

PHYSICAL TRIGGERS:

Yawn first to make your eyes glisten with tears. Take shorter, quicker breaths, and allow your breath to catch slightly. Tense your face muscles, specifically around your eyes and mouth.

SECRET NUMBER 25

HOW TO NOT BLUSH

EVERYBODY THINKS:

If you blush, you blush. And there's nothing you can do about it. Stress or embarrassment makes some people's cheeks turn pink and no one even knows why it happens.

BUT SECRET 25 IS THIS:

When we're embarrassed or stressed our body releases adrenaline, which causes our blood vessels to widen, making our cheeks go redder. Everybody blushes, but paler skin, anxiety and even the fear of blushing can all make it more noticeable.

There are lots of options to help with blushing, including make-up, hypnosis and medicines, but the best place to start is with our magic, two-step solution: Magic Breathing plus Magic Thinking.

PUT IT TO THE TEST:

STEP 1: MAGIC BREATHING

A Magic Double Breath immediately de-stresses you with just two breaths. And that will massively reduce the chances of you blushing. It works like this:

1. Breathe in deeply through your nose…
2. Before you breath out … breathe in again! With a short sharp inbreath.
3. Breathe out slowly.

STEP 2: MAGIC THINKING

Send the blush to your hands instead of your face. That might sound weird, but blood flow can be controlled just using your imagination. Spend five minutes a day imagining your hands heating up around an open fire and you'll find you can more easily direct blood into your hands. Next time you think you might blush, focus on your hands heating up and you'll stop yourself blushing.

HOW TO NOT BLUSH WHEN YOU CALL YOUR TEACHER MUM:
CAN YOU EXPLAIN IT AGAIN, MUM?
FOCUS ON HOT HANDS
DO A MAGIC DOUBLE BREATH

SECRET NUMBER 26

HOW TO UNBLOCK A TOILET

EVERYBODY THINKS:

Blocking a loo is one of the worst things ever, especially if you do it at someone else's house and have to own up. Everybody also thinks they know that the best way to unblock a toilet is to use the toilet brush whilst trying not to breathe.

BUT SECRET 26 IS:

There are much easier ways of unblocking a loo, and they don't end up with a really disgusting loo brush or, worst of all, loo water flicking on your face. *And in your mouth*!

Instead, apply a little science: the science of supermolecules. Washing-up liquid contains molecules with a slippery head and a long, water-hating tail.

When you mix the detergent with water, the water-hating tails group together to "hide" from the water and so the detergent forms into slippery supermolecule balls. That's why washing-up liquid in water is so slippery.

PUT IT TO THE TEST:

Next time you block up the loo, squirt a bit of washing-up liquid down the back and sides of the toilet, so it sinks down into the water.

The slippery supermolecules will form and gradually get between the loo roll and the toilet bowl. Wait as long you can, and then flush. The blockage will slip happily away.

If you just can't wait to test this one out, please see **Secret 27: How to make a floating poo**.

CRET NUMBER 27

HOW TO MAKE A FLOATING POO

EVERYBODY THINKS:

Really? Who wants to know that?

BUT SECRET 27 IS THIS:

The science of poos is fascinating and fundamental to human health. And making a floating poo is surprisingly easy – as long as you're willing to eat a lot of fruit and vegetables. You know that whole five-a-day thing? Think again. We're talking ten-a-day. Yes, you read that right. Ten portions of fruit and veg will put you in the top tier of floating poo producers.

PUT IT TO THE TEST:

STEP 1: EAT TEN PORTIONS OF FRUIT AND VEG IN ONE DAY

A portion size is roughly the amount you can fit in the palm of one hand.

STEP 2: DO A POO!

(You may not have much choice after all that fruit and veg...)

WARNING! If you feel full after a few portions of fruits, STOP.

SECRET NUMBER 28

HOW TO SURVIVE RUNNING OUT OF TOILET ROLL

EVERYBODY THINKS:

If you run out of loo roll, it's the end of the world. Toilet roll is the first thing people panic-buy in a crisis for a reason. And if you happen to be on the toilet when the loo roll runs out … then your life is as good as *over*.

BUT SECRET 28 IS THIS:

Humankind survived for 180 million years without loo roll. Even now, most people on the planet don't use it at all (bidets are used in most of Asia and Southern Europe). And it doesn't even work particularly well. Toilet paper *moves* poo, but it doesn't *remove* it. That probably sounds gross, but the bottom line is: your butt is probably fine with whatever level of microbes and poop are on it right now. We've searched through time and space to uncover the history of clean bums:

CLEAN BUMS THROUGH TIME & SPACE

ANCIENT ROMANS: used a *communal* sponge on a stick[9] (yes, the word communal means everyone shared it).

ANCIENT GREEKS: used broken pieces of pottery. They used the pieces to scrape and wipe as best they could.

EARLY NORTH AMERICAN SETTLERS: used dried corn cobs. They were plentiful, they were soft and they were easy to handle.

INUIT: used snow. Of course they did.

VIKINGS: used rope. No wonder they were so angry!

---

9 Have you ever wondered where the saying, "the wrong end of the stick" came from?

But what do you do when there's no paper in a public toilet? We have questioned some of the world's greatest thinkers to find a fool-proof solution.

PUT IT TO THE TEST:

STEP 1: DON'T PANIC, IT'S NOT DIGNIFIED

STEP 2: CHECK YOUR POCKETS OR BAG

Look for tissues, paper – anything you could use for wiping.

STEP 3: LOOK FOR AN EMPTY CARDBOARD TOILET ROLL

Peel away the outer layers of cardboard to create multiple thin sheets of paper.

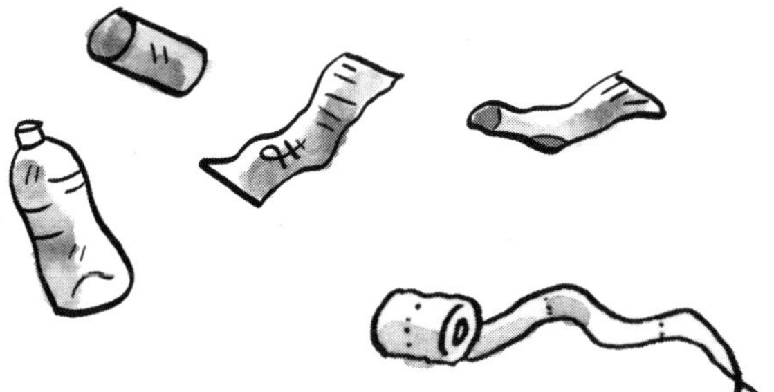

STEP 4: ASK FOR HELP

Swallow your embarrassment and shout. They can just toss a roll over the top of the cubicle.

STEP 5: GOT A BOTTLE OF WATER?

Make yourself a mini bidet. Don't forget to wash your hands.

STEP 6: USE A SOCK

Yes, desperate times call for desperate measures. Sacrifice a sock to the poo gods.

> **BONUS FACT:** The average person uses 85 loo rolls a year, and you'll get through a whole tree by the time you get to about 18 years old.

SECRET NUMBER 29

HOW TO BE BETTER THAN YOUR SIBLING

EVERYBODY THINKS:

It's the worst thing ever when your brother or sister, or even your friend is better than you.

BUT SECRET 29 IS THIS:

It doesn't have to be the worst thing ever. There's always something you'll be best at. The secret is to discover your own skills and talents and find something you enjoy and can shine at.

PUT IT TO THE TEST:

The first thing is to discover if you have any hidden superpowers: see *How to Be a Kid Boss:* **Secret 31: How to discover your hidden superpower.** Then, try this:

FIND YOUR HIDDEN TALENT

THINK: What makes you happy, what do you dream about doing? Write them down.

ASK: Quiz your friends or family. Ask them "What do you think I'd be good at?" then write down their answers.

WISHLIST: Make a note of everything you're interested in.

We've got most things covered in this book and in *How to Be a Kid Boss.* Pick one secret and give it a go.

HOW TO GROW YOUR FINGERS LONGER THAN YOUR LEGS

EVERYBODY THINKS:

Legs are long, fingers are short and there's no way you can grow your fingers longer than your legs.

BUT SECRET 30 IS THIS:

It's not just possible, people have *actually* done it.

You need to understand one (slightly creepy) fact: When you grow your fingernails really long your fingers can grow skin and blood vessels underneath them. This is even more likely if you use false, acrylic nails to help grow your real nails out.

THE WORLD'S LONGEST FINGERNAILS

PUT IT TO THE TEST:

Please don't. For a start, it would make it impossible to pick your nose and then where would you be? (There is no **Secret 102: How to pick your nose with your toe**.) And besides, your nails only grow about 4mm a month, so it would take about 16 years to grow your fingers longer than your legs.

During that time, you'll struggle to do all sorts of useful things – like wipe your bum.

SECRET NUMBER 31

HOW TO TRAIN A LION (OR CAT)

EVERYBODY THINKS:

You can't train a cat. It's harder than pinning jelly to a wall. Get a dog if you want to train a pet or something.[10]

BUT SECRET 31 IS THIS:

Cats can be trained surprisingly easily if you know how. Even though dogs are usually more emotionally intelligent, cats tend to be better problem solvers and have better long-term memory.

And it can help strengthen your bond and prevent your intelligent pet from getting bored.

The secret with cats is to provide a bit of motivation in the form of small treats. You also need a "clicker" so your cat knows exactly when it is getting something right.

HOW TO START

STEP 1: Click and treat *once* to make sure your cat isn't afraid of the sound.

STEP 2: Repeat every time they look at you.

STEP 3: Once your cat understands that their attention results in a click and treat (often in just one session), you can start to increase your distance from them.

STEP 4: As they approach, click and treat. As they eat the treat, move around the room and repeat.

[10] But see also *How to Be a Kid Boss*, **Secret 3: How to train your parents (like a performing seal)**, **Secret 38: How to train a monkey**, and **Secret 79: How to train a slug**.

STEP 5: When your cat comes to you, consistently, add a command word, something like "Come" or "Here" or our favourite, "Meow".

STEP 6: Take it to the next level by calling them from a different room. When they come and find you, click and reward.

DO THIS FOR A FEW MINUTES EVERY DAY AND YOUR CAT WILL SOON GET TO THE POINT WHERE YOU DON'T NEED THE CLICKER ANY MORE.

You're now ready for something more impressive. The Cat High-Five.

PUT IT TO THE TEST:

High-fives look impressive, but are actually easy to teach.

STEP 1: Make sure you and your cat are on a similar eye level. Hold a treat in front of your cat at her shoulder level.

STEP 2: When she reaches out her paw and touches the hand holding the treat, click and give her a treat. Eventually she'll understand she must touch your hand before getting the treat.

STEP 3: At that point, stop holding the treat in the hand you are offering her, and when she touches your hand, click and give her the treat with the other hand.

STEP 4: When she's got the hang of that, start offering your hand in the palm up (high-five) position and give the verbal cue "High five!" When she touches your palm, click and give the reward.

STEP 5: Eventually, as with the other tricks, you will be able to wean her off the clicker and just raise your hand.

Well done, you've cracked it. Give yourself a high-five.

SECRET NUMBER 32

HOW TO CHEAT AT MONOPOLY

EVERYBODY THINKS:

Monopoly is just a game of chance – but there's always someone in any family who takes it weirdly seriously and who seems to win all the time.

BUT SECRET 32 IS THIS:

That person in the family who wins a lot? They're probably cheating.

And maybe it's time for you to be the one in the family who takes it weirdly seriously and wins all the time. Research shows that all billionaires took Monopoly weirdly seriously as a kid.[11] So, if you want to be rich when you grow up, start with Monopoly.

PUT IT TO THE TEST:

You can improve your chances of winning Monopoly by following three simple rules … or, you can cheat. You choose.

DO IT LEGALLY

RULE OF THUMB 1: BUY, BUY, BUY! Buy anything you land on, and buy houses and hotels as soon as you can. You can always trade or mortgage properties later if you need cash. The game is skewed so it favours risk-takers – so be risky.

RULE OF THUMB 2: GO FOR THE RED AND YELLOW PROPERTIES They're the best value.

RULE OF THUMB 3: TRADE! The rules of Monopoly let you do swapsies with other people. Do this *if you possibly can* – because the only way to win is if you get all properties of the same colour. Remember, be nice when you win – don't brag – and people will trade with you next time.

---

[11] OK, our research was rubbish – we only asked two billionaires. But they both took Monopoly way too seriously as kids.

If your little sibling is *still* beating you all the time, it's probably time to cheat. Remember, cheating at Monopoly is practising a valuable life skill, especially if you want to become a secret agent when you grow up.[12]

HOW TO CHEAT

CHEAT 1: The easiest way to cheat is to be in charge of the bank and steal money. But it's easy to get caught (especially if someone empties your pockets before laundry).[13]

CHEAT 2: Each side of the Monopoly board is ten spaces long. So instead of counting each space, get into the habit of jumping ten and then moving either back or forwards for the rest. For example – if you roll 11, jump forwards ten and then move another one. If you roll seven, jump forwards ten and then move back three. After a while, people will stop checking your maths because it makes their brains hurt. *That's when you pounce.* Because no one is checking your maths, you can basically land on Mayfair (or whatever) whenever you want.[14]

[12] See *How to Be a Kid Boss,* **Secret 83: How to become a secret agent**.

[13] This is how I became "Hayes Family Champion" – never losing a game of Monopoly for over a year, between the ages of six and seven (when I was finally caught).

[14] This is how I became the "Hayes Family Champion" – never losing a game of Monopoly in over twenty years, until my family read this book.

SECRET NUMBER 33

HOW TO SLEEP MORE

EVERYBODY THINKS:

There are hundreds of sleep hacks, so obviously they don't work. Because if they did people wouldn't keep inventing more.

You either sleep well or you don't. And good luck getting to sleep on Christmas Eve because that's never gonna happen.

BUT SECRET 33 IS THIS:

Better sleep is big business – we spend over $100 billion on sleep aids every year. And it's obvious why we spend so much: good sleep has some amazing benefits.

BENEFITS OF GOOD SLEEP

But you don't need to spend money. The latest scientific research suggests that the secret to sleeping more comes down to five simple steps.

PUT IT TO THE TEST:

5 STEPS TO DREAMLAND

STEP 1: AVOID SCREENS Blue light from phones and tablets blasts away the sleep hormone, melatonin. So, avoid screens for two full hours before you go to bed.

STEP 2: CONSISTENT BEDTIME
Go to bed at the same time every night … including weekends.

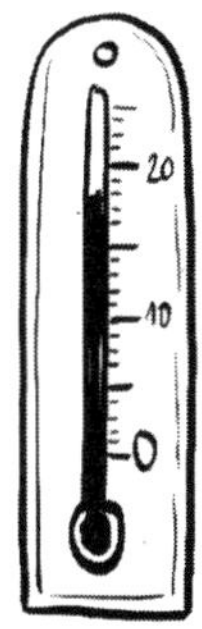

STEP 3: COOL OFF A nice cool bedroom of 18°C is ideal. Even a 1.5 degree increase in that can lose you 44 hours of sleep a year!

STEP 4: BLACKOUT If you don't have blackout blinds, use whatever you can to keep out morning light. People get 25 minutes less sleep in the summer compared to the darker winter.

STEP 5: DON'T JUST LIE THERE WORRYING
Have a pad and pen by your bed and write down anything that's on your mind. And if you're awake in the night for more than thirty minutes, do something relaxing like reading a gentle book or playing Categories (avoid bright lights and screens!).

SECRET NUMBER (34)

HOW TO GET TO SLEEP IN TWO MINUTES

EVERYBODY THINKS:

All you can do is count sheep and hope for the best. And if that doesn't work, then you just have to lie there until dawn, worrying about stuff.

BUT SECRET 34 IS THIS:

During World War II, the US military had a problem. Its pilots were making fatal mistakes because the stress of combat was stopping them sleeping. So, they developed a method to help anyone drop off in two minutes. And best of all, there are just two steps.

PUT IT TO THE TEST:

GET TO SLEEP IN TWO MINUTES *ANYWHERE*

STEP 1: PHYSICALLY RELAX

Breathing deeply and slowly, let each muscle really relax before breathing deeply and moving on to the next. If you struggle to get any body parts relaxed and jellyfish-like, tense them up first, and then let them go loose.

STEP 2: MENTALLY RELAX

Once you're physically relaxed, if you get your mind clear of any active thoughts for just ten seconds, you will be asleep. Imagine you're somewhere still, calm and lovely. Don't allow any other thoughts to creep in...

HOW TO GET OUT OF BED IN THE MORNING

EVERYBODY THINKS:

Getting out of bed in the morning is the hardest thing ever. Especially on a school day. Even an industrial-sized alarm clock won't help.

BUT SECRET 35 IS THIS:

Forget noisy alarm clocks. Even if you hide them on the other side of the room, they'll just make you miserable every morning. And loud alarm clocks have been shown to disrupt sleep cycles and increase sleep anxiety. Here's what to do instead:

HOW TO GET OUT OF BED ON THE RIGHT SIDE

TIP 1: USE A LIGHT ALARM

Or just a bright "cool white" lamp with a timer plug (if you can). The light will remove sleep hormones from your brain.

TIP 2: AS SOON AS YOU WAKE UP, GET OUTSIDE

Or near a bright window. The light will reset your body clock and make it easier to get to sleep (the next evening) and get up (the next day).

TIP 3: GO TO BED AT THE SAME TIME

See also **Secret 33: How to sleep more**.

TIP 4: MOVE TO CALIFORNIA

Where many schools have now changed their start time to 10 o'clock to better fit adolescent children's sleep patterns.[15]

PUT IT TO THE TEST?

Or don't. You probably deserve a lie-in.

---

[15] If this isn't an option, suggest it to your head teacher. The science shows it improves grades and mental health. A school petition wouldn't hurt.

SECRET NUMBER 36

HOW TO MAKE OTHER PEOPLE'S FART SMELL AS NICE AS YOUR OWN

EVERYBODY THINKS:

Their farts smell better than other people's.

BUT SECRET 36 IS THIS:

That can't be true – it's not logically possible. Think about it: we can't all hav nicer-smelling farts than other people.

So, what's going on?

Everyone's farts are unique because our particular mix of gut bacteria is unique, with up to a thousand different species living there and belching out ga

So, with all those bacteria, it's no surprise that we fart a lot: on average, about fourteen times a day. Adults produce about half a litre of fart per day. Some scientists think this means we become "habituated" to our own farts, which means we're so used to smelling them that we barely notice them. But in nature, survival depends on your ability to notice smells that could represent danger or disease, so our brains have evolved to notice new stinky smells.

EVOLUTION IN ACTION: HOW WE EVOLVED TO HATE OTHER PEOPLE'S FARTS

[16] Try not to think about it. If you do, think about this instead: it would take the population of Paris one minute to fill up a hot air balloon with farts.

And that's why other people's farts smell worse than our own.

So, is there anything we can do about it? Well in theory, yes. To some extent you can change your gut bacteria – just by changing what you eat. People who eat similar food to you (like your family) are likely to have similar smelling farts which smell "better".

PUT IT TO THE TEST:

Or don't. We didn't. But if you really want to, next time someone in your family farts, score it out of 100 on this Disgusto Meter. Then do the same for a friend who eats very different food to you.

THE DISGUSTO METER

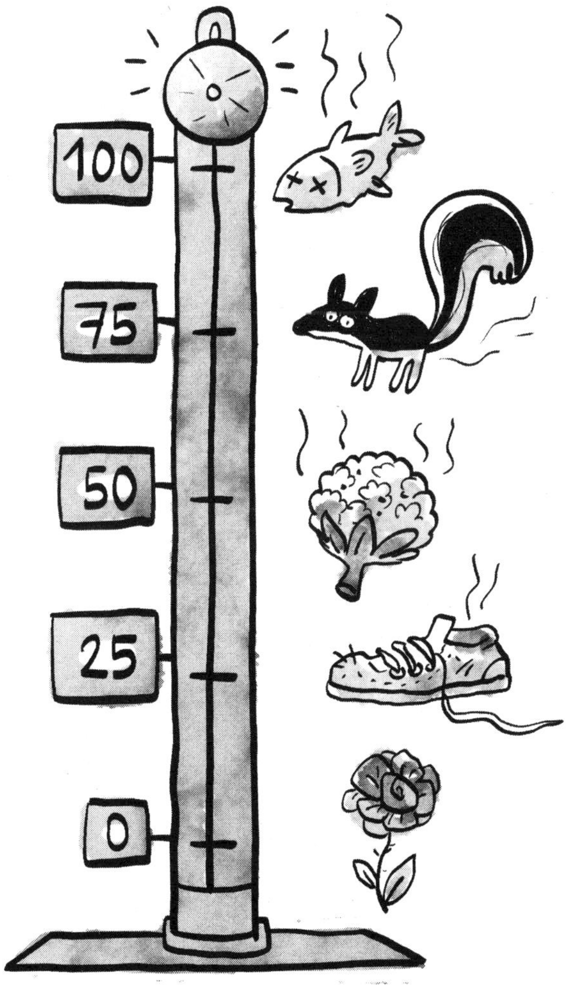

SECRET NUMBER 37

HOW TO DODGE CHORES

EVERYBODY THINKS:

Life is hard and there's no avoiding chores. When adults realize you can tidy up Lego or work a vacuum cleaner, you're totally doomed. For the rest of your life there'll be shouting and complaining and rotas and you'll never be left in peace ever again.

BUT SECRET 37 IS THIS:

Although it's impossible to avoid *all* the chores *all* of the time – you can avoid most chores most of the time. You just need a three-pronged approach:

STEP 1: REDUCE UNNECESSARY CHORES.

STEP 2: AVOID MISERABLE CHORES.

STEP 3: EMBRACE THE CHORES THAT AREN'T TOO BAD.

PUT IT TO THE TEST:

HOW TO DODGE CHORES:

1. REDUCE: Most chores don't need to be done. Help your grown-ups see the light.

2. AVOID: Everyone has a list of chores they really hate. Do them badly and you won't be asked again. But make sure you do something else instead...

3. EMBRACE: If you *like* doing something, it's not a chore. So, if you don't mind walking the dog – make that your thing.

SUPER CHEAT: Volunteer to do *all the vacuuming* and then buy a robot vacuum (you'll need money, see **Secret 51: How to make money when you're still at school**).

If none of the above works then try doing your chores in half the time. See **Secret 38: How to tidy faster**.

HOW TO TIDY FASTER

EVERYBODY THINKS:

Tidying is boring and takes ages.

BUT SECRET 38 IS THIS:

They're only half right. It needn't take ages. If this ever happens to you, then don't worry – because there's a simple seven-point solution:

PUT IT TO THE TEST:

THE SIMPLE SEVEN-POINT SOLUTION:

1. Set a timer for 15 minutes.
2. Get a carrier bag and fill it with any rubbish, then put that in the bin.
3. Put all the dirty laundry in the laundry basket.
4. Make your bed.
5. Get another carrier bag and put any remaining stuff/mess in it.
6. Empty the carrier bag by putting the stuff where it belongs.
7. If there's any stuff left in the bag when the alarm goes off – don't worry. Just hide the bag somewhere and get back to your life.

SECRET NUMBER 39

HOW TO WRITE AN IMPORTANT EMAIL OR LETTER

EVERYBODY THINKS:

Emails and letters are only for old people.

BUT SECRET 39 IS THIS:

Humans send 392 billion emails every day, and about 250 billion letters. Odds are, at some point, you're going to have to send one. But here's the kicker: of all those emails, only about one in seven is actually read.

Writing *compelling* emails and letters is a superpower most adults would love to have. It might seem like the world's most boring superpower, but it's not.[17] An effective email or letter is a magic key for making other people do stuff you want: give you money, toys,[18] a job or a promotion. Here's how to superpower up:

PUT IT TO THE TEST:

1. **GREETING:** Make a good first impression by choosing the right salutation. "Hi" and "Hello" are OK if you know the person. Only use "Dear…" for letters or a very formal email, like a new job application. If you don't know how someone prefers to be addressed, use their full name.
2. **GOAL:** Decide exactly what you want from the person you're writing to.
3. **GET TO THE POINT:** A bit of friendly stuff is OK, but don't overdo it.
4. **AVOID:** Emoticons, emojis and acronyms unless you really know someone well.
5. **SIGN OFF:** Stick to the basics. Sincerely, Many Thanks, Best, Best Regards, and Best Wishes are all fine.
6. **CHECK IT:** Read it out loud before you send and use a "grammar checker" if you need to.

---

[17] The world's most boring superpower is being able to eat broccoli without flinching (see *How to Be a Kid Boss*, **Secret 82: How to eat broccoli**).

[18] See also *How to Be a Kid Boss*, **Secret 76: How to do whatever you want**.

HOW TO PACK A SUITCASE

EVERYBODY THINKS:

Packing is hard. That's why you get your grown-ups to do it. And even *they* get stressed and forget your asthma inhaler or swimming trunks.

BUT SECRET 40 IS THIS:

Just seven rules will get you to packing utopia. Follow these and you'll be able to pack quickly and stress free.

1. **PACKING LIST:** Search online for packing lists for your specific trip (e.g., "packing list for a four-night school trip"). Change it so it's right for you.

2. **CLOTHES:** Plan your outfits each day by laying them out on your bed. Common mistakes are: not packing anything waterproof and forgetting your pyjamas. And pack a small cloth bag to put your dirty laundry in.

3. **SHOES:** Always have more than one pair. Even if it's just flip flops.

4. **TOILETRIES & MEDICINE:** Yes, make sure that inhaler goes on the list in BLOCK CAPITALS.

5. **GADGETS:** The most common thing people forget to pack is a charger.[19]

6. **LEAVE SOME ROOM:** Don't pack fit to bursting.

7. **DON'T SWEAT IT:** If you forget something, it's not the end of the world. You can always make that pair of pants last a week (if you really need to).

PUT IT TO THE TEST:

If you want to practise before a big trip, try doing a dummy run. Pack a suitcase for the school week, then try to live out of the suitcase for five days. You'll soon discover what you forgot.

---

[19] According to the same research, the second most common thing to be forgotten is toothpaste.

SECRET NUMBER 41

HOW TO DO TWO THINGS AT ONCE

EVERYBODY THINKS:

It's impossible to do two things at once. You just end up failing at both. Your brain is like an old computer and if you run too many programs at once, it just crashes. If you don't believe me, then try saying the alphabet backwards whilst juggling an egg.

BUT SECRET 41 IS THIS:

Everybody can multitask. And that's great, because otherwise planes would crash every time the pilot needed to hold in a fart and fly at the same time.

The problem is that we're *less* good when we do it. Studies show we lose about fifteen IQ points when we try to do two things at once. And not only do we make more mistakes, multitasking wastes time and makes us more stressed. So, avoid multitasking whenever you can.

HOW TO AVOID MULTITASKING:

TURN OFF NOTIFICATIONS on all devices and give yourself an instant IQ boost.

SET A TIME LIMIT for each task and then switch. Need to practise guitar and revise? Do each in twenty-minute chunks to enjoy the maximum benefits of both.

DO MORE EXERCISE to improve focus. Take a five-minute physical break between jobs.

But it's not *always* possible to avoid multitasking, especially at work or school. Luckily, the science also shows that you can train yourself to be better at multi-tasking. And best of all, all you need to do is play video games.

PUT IT TO THE TEST:

STEP 1: TEST

Find someone who doesn't play video games and time them doing this challenge:

NAME FORTY ANIMALS WHILST EATING TWENTY BAKED BEANS WITH A COCKTAIL STICK.

STEP 2: PLAY

Get them to play fast-action video games for a total of twelve hours over the next month.

STEP 3: TEST AGAIN

See how their multitasking ability has improved.

> **BONUS FACT:**
>
> Not all double tasking is bad. Sometimes two things go really well together.
>
> **STUDYING AND MUSIC:** Instrumental music can help you learn faster.
>
> **EXERCISE AND CREATIVITY:** If you need ideas, go for a run or walk.
>
> **PODCASTS AND BORING STUFF:** A good podcast can even make the washing-up less soul-crushingly boring.

SECRET NUMBER 42

HOW TO DO YOUR OWN LAUNDRY

EVERYBODY THINKS:

Doing the laundry is complicated and if you get it wrong, you'll end up feeling a bit stressed.

BUT SECRET 42 IS THIS:

Even though there are seven rules to doing the laundry, luckily each one has a cheat.

THE 7 RULES OF LAUNDRY AND HOW TO CHEAT

RULE 1: READ THE LABEL

Check the maximum temperature. Ignore everything else, no one knows what all those hieroglyphics mean.

CHEAT 1:

Wash everything on 30°C.

RULE 2: SEPARATE YOUR CLOTHES

Into whites, light and dark colours.

CHEAT 2:

Use a colour collector sheet and wash everything together

RULE 3: DON'T OVERFILL

Every washing machine has a maximum weight of clothes.

CHEAT 3:

Leave a 10cm gap from the top of the laundry to the top of the door.

RULE 4: PUT THE DETERGENT IN THE CORRECT DRAWER

Make sure it goes in the little drawer on the left.

CHEAT 4:

Just stick the detergent in the main drum on top of the clothes.

RULE 5: DON'T TUMBLE DRY

Unless is has a label with a symbol that shows a square with a cirle inside. And don't iron without following the setting on the label.

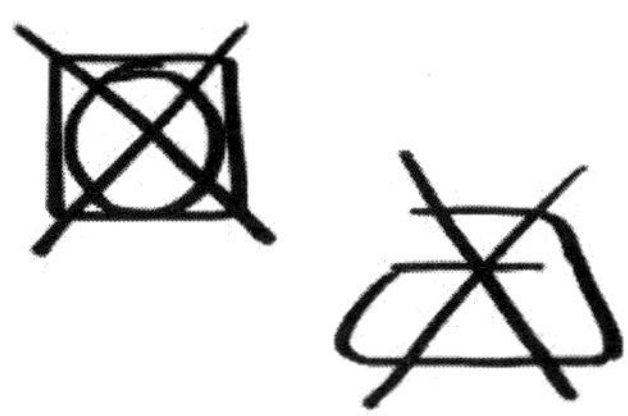

CHEAT 5:

Don't tumble dry or iron anything, ever.

RULE 6: BE EXTRA CAREFUL WITH OTHER PEOPLE'S CLOTHES

CHEAT 6:

Never wash other people's clothes. It always ends badly.

PUT IT TO THE TEST:

Or don't – just let your grown-ups do it.

HOW TO CHOOSE YOUR CLOTHES

EVERYBODY THINKS:

Choosing a style that suits you is really hard, and probably best left to the experts: people really into clothes and fashion. For the rest of us we should try to wear what everyone else is wearing so we blend in. Or maybe just copy a style from a group we want to join.

BUT SECRET 43 IS THIS:

Figuring out your look can be tricky. How you look isn't as important as what you're like, but it's still important. If you look good, you'll feel good.

The "right" clothes may suit your body shape, be comfortable, look good, be on trend, be affordable and keep your parents happy. That sounds like an impossible nightmare, but don't worry – with a few simple tips, developing a style can be fun. When it comes to choosing clothes, the internet is your best friend – here's how.

PUT IT TO THE TEST:

1. KEEP IT PERSONAL

Match your clothes to your personality. Write down five words that describe what you're like or what you like. Then image search for clothes that fit that person.

2. FIND TRENDS
Find out what's on trend by searching "on trend clothes" then insert the season and year.

3. COPY CLOTHES
If someone is wearing clothes you like – do a "Reverse Image Search" to find similar clothes. This can also help you source cheaper versions.

4. THINK HOW YOU BUY
If possible, buy clothes in person at shops to ensure size/fit. If buying online, ensure whatever shop you use is trusted, with good reviews, has a simple returns policy and that the pieces you buy are durable – go for quality over quantity.

5. KEEP YOUR PARENTS HAPPY
Search "Why you should let children choose their own clothes".

SECRET NUMBER 44

HOW TO DRESS YOURSELF HAPPY

EVERYBODY THINKS:

Clothes can't make you happy. Usually they're a source of stress ("What should I wear?"), or boredom (school uniform) or laundry.

BUT SECRET 44 IS THIS:

You can follow the science on this one. Studies have revealed how wearing different clothes can change our mood, energy and the levels of feel-good chemicals in our brains.

Colour and fit plays a big part, but so do memories and associations and even the "personality type" of the clothes we wear.

FOUR EASY WAYS TO DRESS YOURSELF HAPPY:

1. USE COLOUR PSYCHOLOGY

Studies suggest that yellow, pink and red have an uplifting, energizing effect on our mood. On the other side of the rainbow are short wavelength colours, such as blue, purple and indigo. These colours are perfect to wear if you want to be creative, get focused or wind down.

2. WEAR ACTIVEWEAR

When we feel low, we tend to go for baggy clothing, like hoodies. But research says we should do the opposite. A slight squeezing sensation around the body has an instant impact on our mood – like a soothing hug that calms down the nervous system. Try activewear. You can always wear that baggy hoodie over the top.

3. WEAR OLD FAVOURITES

Clothes are like memory banks. They can be powerful triggers of happy times.

4. LOOK GOOD, FEEL GOOD!

Look in the mirror and ask yourself some questions, such as: what is required of me today? How do I want to feel today? What side of me do I want to celebrate? Then decide if what you're wearing lines up with the answers to those questions. Check out **Secret 43: How to choose your clothes**.

PUT IT TO THE TEST:

Test it out with a quick experiment. Try an exercise challenge, like how many burpees you can do in one minute. Do it once wearing a red or bright pink T-shirt, then try it wearing purple or blue.

HOW TO NOT BE A MOSQUITO MAGNET

EVERYBODY THINKS:

There are two kinds of people in the world. There are those who can spend hours outdoors without getting bitten by mosquitos, and then there a "Mosquito Magnets". If you happen to be a mosquito magnet, bad luck, there's nothing you can do to avoid this.

BUT SECRET 45 IS THIS:

A new discovery by scientists has revealed why mosquitos go for some people more than others – it's all because of the smell of your skin. And it comes down to two chemicals:

1. MOSQUITO MAGNET
Skin smells of carboxylic acid, the chemical found in punchy cheeses.

2. MOSQUITO PROOF
Skin smells of eucalyptols, the chemical found in plants like basil, sage and rosemary.

BONUS FACT: Mosquitos are part of the fly family, and usually feed on nectar. However, females preparing to produce eggs need a meal with extra protein: your blood.

PUT IT TO THE TEST:

Mosquito bites can spread disease so you should always do whatever you can to avoid getting bitten: insect repellent, long clothing, mosquito nets and fans. But you can also give yourself a head start by changing what you eat. You can change the smell of your skin by avoiding stinky cheese, and eating plenty of rosemary, sage, basil and cardamon.

And if you can't do that, there's always eucalyptus toothpaste...

PRO TIP: Avoid eating bananas – they'll turn anyone into a mosquito magnet.

SECRET NUMBER 46

HOW TO MAKE YOURSELF HAPPIER WITH A PENCIL

EVERYBODY THINKS:

That pencils won't make you happier. Unless, of course, you've ever had a broken arm in a plaster cast. In which case you can use a pencil to scratch an itchy wrist.

BUT SECRET 46 IS THIS:

You don't need to break your arm first. A pencil can make anyone happier. Just put it between your teeth (sideways on) and it will force your mouth into a smile. Your brain will do the rest.

> **WARNING!** Don't put either end of the pencil in your mouth – just hold the pencil between your teeth. And if it starts to hurt, stop.

This works because of one simple fact: being happy makes you smile, but it also works the other way round, smiling tends to make you happier.

It works because of something called **PRIMING**: your brain is wired up so that if it feels you smiling it gets ready to notice funny or happy things. Weird, huh?

Well don't just sit there frowning, try it!

PUT IT TO THE TEST:

MAKE YOURSELF HAPPIER WITH A PENCIL

STEP 1: Put the pencil between your teeth like this:

STEP 2: Wait 60 seconds...

STEP 3: Feel happier.

HOW TO PASS EXAMS WITHOUT WORKING UP A SWEAT

EVERYBODY THINKS:

Exams are hard and miserable.

BUT SECRET 47 IS THIS:

You can make them a lot easier with these five exam hacks.

EXAM HACK 1: PRACTICE QUESTIONS

Forget revising, just learn by doing questions. Using an app for instant feedback will rocket fuel your progress and can help you learn at more than double speed.[20]

EXAM HACK 2: DO THE MAGIC DOUBLE BREATH

Breathe for instant anxiety relief (see **Secret 25: How to not blush**).

EXAM HACK 3: EXERCISE

This is the best way to relieve exam stress. It also improves memory and can add 10 points to your IQ.

EXAM HACK 4: DRINK WATER

A hydrated brain can remember about 25% better and faster. And in cognitive tests, hydrated people typically make half as many errors.

EXAM HACK 5: CHEW GUM

For an instant destresser. Scientific studies also suggest that chewing gum can boost your IQ and memory. Just don't swallow it.[21]

EXAM HACK 6: SLEEP

For better memory and brain power (see **Secret 34: How to get to sleep in two minutes**).

---

[20] Your teachers will know the best apps for your specific exams. And also, make sure you practise essay and long form questions too. If there's anything you don't understand, ask your teacher – they really do want to help!

[21] But if you do see **Secret 20: How to survive swallowing bubblegum**.

SECRET NUMBER 48

HOW TO READ A MAP

EVERYBODY THINKS:

Only old people use maps, everyone else has GPS on their phone.

BUT SECRET 48 IS THIS:

When zombies overrun the planet in 2038 and phones stop working, you'll want to know how to read a map quickly. Maybe even really, *really* quickly ... so it's best to learn now. This also works when your battery is flat. Finding north is the big secret; get that right and everything else is easy. But what if you don't have a compass?

WHERE'S NORTH?

If you have a watch, you're in luck.

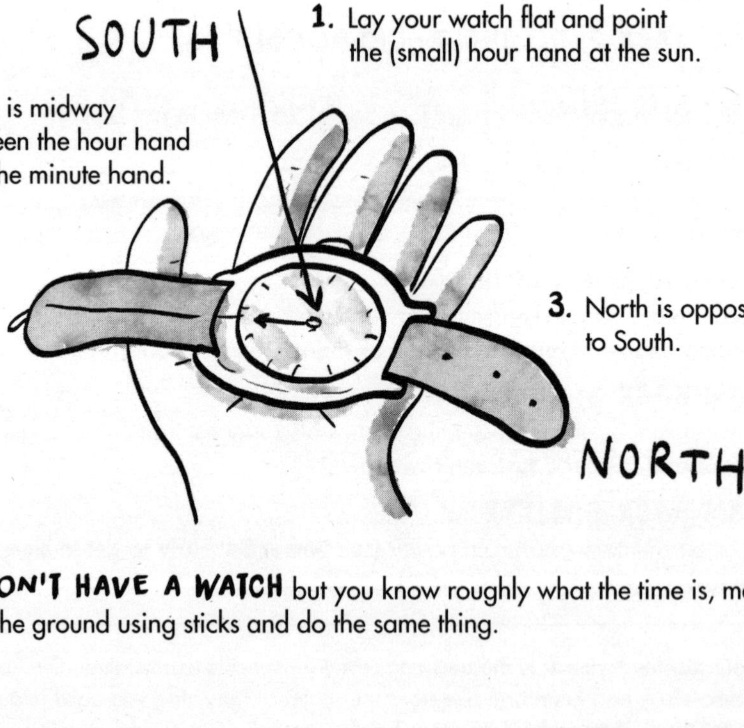

1. Lay your watch flat and point the (small) hour hand at the sun.
2. South is midway between the hour hand and the minute hand.
3. North is opposite to South.

IF YOU DON'T HAVE A WATCH but you know roughly what the time is, make a watch on the ground using sticks and do the same thing.

IF IT'S DARK find the Polaris: the bright, pole star. First, find the Big Dipper. It looks like a big ladle on its side. The two stars on the Dipper's "cup" point to Polaris, which is the tip of the handle of the Little Dipper (looks like a little ladle on its side).

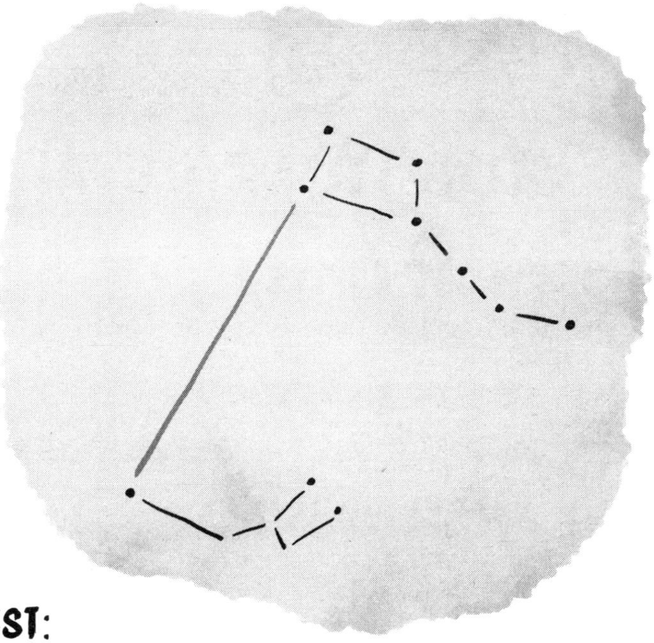

PUT IT TO THE TEST:

MAP READING SURVIVAL GUIDE

MAP TIP 1: POINT THE MAP NORTH

Easy!

MAP TIP 2: DISTANCE

Figure out the scale on your map, so you know roughly how far away things are.[22] On a hike, the average person normally walks about one kilometre every ten minutes, so if you're running from a zombie, it could take as little as five minutes.

MAP TIP 3: RECOGNIZE KEY FEATURES

Use your map to identify landmarks you'll see along the way. It could be a church or a building or river. Plot your journey by going from one landmark to the next.

MAP TIP 4: LEARN TO READ THE RED "CONTOUR" LINES

This is *elite-level* map reading. Hills and mountains are often the best landmarks. The red lines on the map show you the height and shape of the ground. Look for the little closed loop in the middle of lots of red contour lines – that's the top of a hill or mountain.

---

[22] If the scale is given as a ratio then it can be quite tricky. For example 1:100,000, means that every 1cm on the map represents 100,000cm on the ground (100,000cm = 1 km!). Usually there's also a little ruler. Put your finger on it and see how many km the width of your finger is worth.

SECRET NUMBER 49

HOW TO GIVE A SPEECH

EVERYBODY THINKS:

Only really confident people can give good speeches. The rest of us will just die on stage and it will be awful. Better to just avoid the whole thing.

BUT SECRET 49 IS THIS:

Anyone can give a good speech. It all comes down to practice and knowing a few genius tips and tricks. Sooner or later, everyone has to stand up and talk in front of other people.

If just the thought of giving a speech fills you with dread and horror, practise dummy runs in your bedroom.

But first up, you need to write the thing…

HOW TO WRITE A SPEECH

COPY: Don't be afraid to copy other people's ideas. The internet is your friend. Need a joke to introduce yourself? Google it.

WRITE IT OUT: Word-for-word, exactly as you plan on saying it. But don't read it if you can avoid it – just use it for a quick check if you forget something.

KEEP IT SHORT: Five minutes is better than fifteen. We speak about 140 words a minute, so decide how many minutes you want to speak for and then stick to your word count.

START WITH A JOKE: If you're nervous, make the joke about how nervous you are. Search for "icebreaker jokes about being nervous" online.

PICK YOUR THEME AND STICK TO IT! If you had to say what your speech is about in one sentence, what would it be? That's your theme.

BACK IT UP: Back up your theme with three or four points. Try to make at least one of these points using a story.

THROW IN A RHETORICAL QUESTION: To get the listeners' attention, and then answer it yourself.

KILLER FINISH: Funny is good, but failing that, just go with a simple thank you.

So, you've finished writing; now, you just have to perform it. Don't panic, you've got this.

PUT IT TO THE TEST:

HOW TO PERFORM YOUR SPEECH

PRACTISE: It won't make perfect, but it will make it easier. Practise over and over. By the time you actually give the speech your brain will be so bored it might even forget to panic.

IMAGINE THE WORST THING THAT CAN HAPPEN: Maybe you forget what you're saying. Now think of something to say in case that does happen. It doesn't have to be funny – you'll get a laugh just for saying, "I knew this would happen!"

RELAX: We know it's not easy to relax before a speech, but you can instantly breathe away some nerves with a "Magic Double Breath" (see **Secret 25: How to not blush**).

EYE CONTACT: This can be hard to do too. But if there's a friendly face or two in the audience, give them a smile early on. Their smile back will work wonders.

SPEAK SLOOOOWWWWLYYY: Time yourself when you practise and try to keep under that golden 140 words per minute.

That's it. This time next year, you'll be Prime Minister.

SECRET NUMBER 50

HOW TO SAY NO

EVERYBODY THINKS:

If you say, "no" to someone it will end badly. You'll either annoy them, disappoint them, or you'll miss out on something. Life's easier if you just say "yes" all the time.

BUT SECRET 50 IS THIS:

Being able to say no is a major life skill – it will help reduce stress and give you time and energy for what's really important. So don't feel guilty, and don't worry they'll stop liking you. Just learn how to do it in a clear and kind way that earns you respect.

UNDERSTAND WHY IT FEELS HARD

Saying no can make you feel guilty or worry about upsetting people. Remember: if you're clear, kind and reasonable, a good person will usually think better of you for saying no. And if the person is really your friend, they'll understand!

BE CRYSTAL CLEAR

Don't be wishy-washy, practise saying a few nice phrases: "Sadly, I can't" or "I'm sorry, but I'm not able to."

EXPLAIN YOURSELF BUT SKIP LONG EXCUSES

"I can't because I've got an important football match" is enough, you don't need to go on and on.

OFFER AN ALTERNATIVE

But only if you can and want to.

PUT IT TO THE TEST:

HERE'S A COMMON SCENARIO WHERE THE PRESSURE IS ON TO SAY YES:

SECRET NUMBER 51

HOW TO MAKE MONEY WHEN YOU'RE STILL AT SCHOOL

EVERYBODY THINKS:

You can't make money when you're just a kid. After all, you're just a kid.

BUT SECRET 51 IS THIS:

Yeah, you can – you just need a *side hustle*. And we have plenty.

PUT IT TO THE TEST:

Make sure you have a trusted grown-up in cahoots with you, but don't let them take a portion of your profits!

MAKE SOME DOSH

---

[23] For genius tips, see *How to Be a Kid Boss,* **Secret 16: How to make loads of money**.

[24] You can earn double minimum wage. See *How to Be a Kid Boss,* **Secret 54: How to ace your exams**.

[25] See **Secret 65: How to win loads of stuff**.

[26] See *How to Be a Kid Boss,* **Secret 34: How to invent something**.

HOW TO FIND SOMETHING YOU'VE LOST

EVERYBODY THINKS:

That if they say, "Where did you last have it?" you'll magically be able to find lost things.

BUT SECRET 52 IS THIS:

The sentence, "Where did you last have it?" is the most annoying sentence in the English language. But scientists have discovered the secrets to finding lost stuff, and it could save you time for the rest of your life.

HOW TO FIND LOST STUFF

STEP 1: DON'T LOOK FOR IT

The most common mistake is to start hunting immediately and in a random, increasingly frenzied way. Instead, think for ten seconds where it might be.

STEP 2: THE TWO CS

Keep calm and confident. If you calm down, the location of the lost object will often magically float up in your mind.

STEP 3: GO BACK TO WHERE YOU FIRST LOOKED

Usually, you just missed it first time around.

STEP 4: MOVE THINGS

Look in the most cluttered places and tidy them up a bit. Moving things is the number one top tip. Look with your hands as well as your eyes.

STEP 5: RETRACE YOUR STEPS

Yes, sorry about this, but do try and remember where you last had it.

PUT IT TO THE TEST:

Looking is a skill. And like all skills, it gets better with practice.

SECRET NUMBER 53

HOW TO NOT LOSE YOUR TEMPER

EVERYBODY THINKS:

Anger is a *bad* emotion, and losing your temper is a really, really terrible thing to do. Even when your little brother upsets your hamster.

BUT SECRET 53 IS THIS:

It's not bad to feel angry. Anger is a normal, healthy emotion. In fact, loads of really good things come from anger. Revolutionary thinkers like Susan B. Anthony and Martin Luther King Jr used their anger about injustices to make the world a better place. But uncontrolled anger can be a big problem. So how do you own your anger, and control it in a healthy way?

WHAT DOESN'T WORK?

VENTING: Punching your pillow, screaming and trashing the room doesn't actually "release" pent-up rage. In fact, research suggests that the more you vent, the worse you'll feel.

IGNORING IT: Denying your angry feelings, or allowing others to treat you badly has been linked to a variety of physical and mental health issues, from hypertension to depression.

WHAT DOES WORK?

EXPRESSING IT: The best way to deal with anger is to find a healthy way to say what you're feeling.

FIXING IT: Turn anger into something constructive. Be assertive about what you want to happen, without being aggressive.

Staying in control when you feel angry is easier said than done. So, we found the **TOP FOUR TEMPER TIPS** for managing your anger. The more you practise these Temper Tips, the better you'll control things when you do get angry.

PUT IT TO THE TEST:

TEMPER TIP 1: SPOT THE SIGNS

Practise noticing when you feel frustrated, disappointed, or downright angry.

TEMPER TIP 2: GIVE YOURSELF A BREATHER

We recommend the Magic Double Breath:[27]

STEP 1: Breathe in deeply through your nose,

STEP 2: Before you breath out … breathe in again! With a short sharp second inbreath.

STEP 3: Breathe out slowly.

TEMPER TIP 3: SAY IT!

Be loud and proud about what you're feeling. Just saying: "I feel so angry about this"can help.

TEMPER TIP 4: LOOK FOR A SOLUTION

Explaining what you want to happen (even if it is only to yourself) is the first step to bringing the change you need.

---

[27] It also stops hiccups, laughter, blushing and reduces anxiety. See also **Secret 16: How to ot laugh when someone farts** and **Secret 25: How to not blush**.

SECRET NUMBER 54

HOW TO SURVIVE ON JUST CHOCOLATE

EVERYBODY THINKS:

You can't survive on just chocolate. It's mainly sugar and even before the sugar kills you, you'll die of thirst. The rule of thumb is: you can only survive without water for about three days. So that's about your limit if you insist on just surviving on chocolate from now on.

BUT SECRET 54 IS THIS:

You can always drink chocolate milkshakes! That could give you plenty of liquid.

Unfortunately, the next thing to worry about is the sugar. The recommended maximum amount of free sugar for a child is 24g (six sugar cubes) a day. If you just ate chocolate all day, you'd eat about 200g of sugar (fifty sugar cubes!). At that level you can probably expect to die within a few months.

But weirdly, the thing that will actually kill you soonest is the lack of protein. Chocolate doesn't contain all the different types of protein you need, and so muscle loss will kick in after about 24 hours.

So is it possible to survive on just chocolate, or what? Yes, it is (sort of), but you need to cheat a bit by adding chocolate to other foods so you get enough fibre, protein and other nutrients to keep you healthy. Here's how...

> **WARNING!** If you can't eat a lot of sugar or have any allergies to any of the food in the meal plan, just skip this secret. But don't worry, there are still another 100 other secrets to choose from!

PUT IT TO THE TEST:

CHOCOLATE DAY MEAL PLAN

You will need some drinking chocolate powder[28] and jar of chocolate and hazelnut spread.

BREAKFAST: Avoid chocolate cereals. Instead, add 2 teaspoons of chocolate powder to porridge or a sugar free cereal, though porridge is best. **[Sugar = 6g]**

DRINKS: You need to drink about six cups of liquid a day. Three cups can be in the form of milk. So the answer is to have six cups of drinking chocolate made of half milk, half water. Make it weak with only 2 teaspoons of chocolate powder so you don't blow your entire free sugar allowance. **[Sugar = 6g]**

LUNCH: CHOCO CHEESE TOASTIE

Chocolate spread and cheese go surprisingly well together, especially mozzarella. Make a cheese toastie with your favourite cheese and add a teaspoon of chocolate spread onto the cheese.

CHOCOLATE NUT MUSH: Add 1 teaspoon of chocolate spread to a mix of smashed-up nuts. Eat it with a spoon.
CHOCOLATE STRAWBERRIES: Dip a strawberry into 1 teaspoon of chocolate spread. **[Sugar = 9g]**

SUPPER/DINNER: CHOCOLATE SPAGHETTI BOLOGNESE

Add one teaspoon of chocolate powder per person to the spag-bol sauce. This is an Italian tradition that goes way back and it's surprisingly tasty – adding a richness which really brings out the flavour. **[Sugar = 3g]**

Congratulations, you ate chocolate all day!

---

[28] Find a brand that has less than 60g of sugar per 100g of powder.

HOW TO BE A CHAMPION CHEF

EVERYBODY THINKS:

That becoming a champion chef takes 10,000 hours sweating away in a kitchen while other angry chefs scream insults at you:

BUT SECRET 55 IS THIS:

Genius chef hacks will get you well on the way to becoming a cooking champion.

CHEF HACKS

Tie your apron and master these six hacks! Just remember to get an adult to show you how to do the hacks safely.

HACK 1: MASTER THE 5 BASICS

Get someone to show you how to:

1. Chop an onion (get an adult to show you how to do this safely!).
2. Peel a carrot.
3. Dress a salad.
4. Cook an omelette.
5. Make a sauce (tomato or béchamel, whichever you like best). Search online for a video if you need to.

HACK 2: READ THE WHOLE RECIPE

Before you start. Make sure you have all the ingredients and all the equipment you need.

HACK 3: ADD EXTRA BUTTER

If the recipe calls for butter, add a bit extra to improve the "mouth feel" of the food.

HACK 4: COOK WHAT YOU LOVE

But try it with a twist. If you like pasta sauces, try making a bit of basil oil to give it some star appeal. Search online for the "Michelin star version of..." your favourite recipe.

HACK 5: HAVE HERO INGREDIENTS

Every chef needs a hero ingredient to drizzle over the finished dish and give it star appeal. Two to try are "pomegranate molasses" and a balsamic vinegar "reduction".[29]

HACK 6: MAKE IT ART

"Plating up" is the most important hack of all. If you wow someone's eyes, you're more than halfway to wowing their tastebuds. The five top tips are:

1. Create height on the plate
2. Lots of colours
3. Big plates
4. Small portions
5. For specific ideas, search the "world's most beautiful..." version of your favourite recipe.

PUT IT TO THE TEST:

Check out **Secret 56: How to make "the perfection burger"** and **Secret 57: How to make the world's best pancakes.**

---

[29] That just means pouring some balsamic vinegar into a pan and cooking it for 10 minutes on a low heat until it goes thick, gooey and sugary.

HOW TO MAKE "THE PERFECTION BURGER"

EVERYBODY THINKS:

You have to be a top chef to make epic food.

BUT SECRET 56 IS THIS:

Having a perfect recipe means you can make the perfect burger!

PUT IT TO THE TEST:

Cook your perfection burgers and watch the astonished faces of friends and family as you serve them THE BEST BURGER EVER!!!

"THE PERFECTION BURGER"

INGREDIENTS:

- 1 tablespoon butter[30]
- 1 large onion (finely chopped)
- 500g beef mince (or 2 tins of black beans, drained)[31]
- 1 egg (beaten with a fork)
- 2 tablespoons breadcrumbs
- 2 teaspoons parsley (finely chopped)
- A pinch of salt & black pepper
- 6 burger buns

OPTIONAL EXTRAS:

- Slices of cheese (Brie, Cheddar, Gouda or preferred dairy-free alternative)
- A handful of lettuce leaves
- Thinly sliced red onion and gherkins
- Burger sauce (my personal favourite mix is equal parts ketchup + balsamic vinegar + chilli sauce)

---

[30] For the world's best VEGAN BURGER, replace butter with olive oil and the egg with a "chia egg" (1 tablespoon of chia seeds soaked in 3 tablespoons of water for 5 minutes until it goes gooey).

[31] For a delicious veggie version, add a tablespoon of olive oil to the black beans and roast the burgers on a baking tray for 25 minutes at 180°C.

RECIPE

1. Heat the butter in a frying pan over a low heat, and cook the onion until soft and *slightly* browned. Leave to cool.

2. Tip the beef into a mixing bowl (or add the drained black beans to a mixing bowl) and sprinkle over the onion. Add the egg, breadcrumbs, herbs and seasoning and mix together gently with a fork.

3. Divide the mix into six balls, then shape into flattish burgers, putting a dimple in the centre of each. Put the burgers on a baking tray, cover and put in the fridge for an hour.

4. Ask an adult to help you carefully transfer the burgers to a medium-hot pan. Leave them for the first three minutes to build up a good seal on the bottom then carefully turn them over, adding cheese on top if desired.

5. Cook for a further seven minutes. While you're waiting, ask your adult to cut and lightly toast the burger buns.

6. Create your burger work of art.

7. For maximum enjoyment, look at it for at least a minute before you dig in. It will be the best burger you ever eat!

WARNING! As we know, kitchens and cooking can be tricky, so make sure you have a grown-up on hand to help you with the difficult bits. If you have food allergies or are cooking for someone, you need to check the ingredients list carefully.

HOW TO MAKE THE WORLD'S BEST PANCAKES

EVERYBODY THINKS:

To make the best pancakes in the world you need to train for years, being shouted at by some angry chef with a Michelin star.

BUT SECRET 57 IS THIS:

You can make fluffy and squidgy pancakes worthy of a Michelin star with just a few tricks and they look impressive!

PUT IT TO THE TEST:

FLUFFY AND SQUIDGY

The secret here is to use buttermilk and bicarbonate of soda. The acid in the buttermilk reacts with the bicarbonate of soda to fluff them up and it breaks down the protein in the flour to make them melt in the mouth – delicious![32]

---

[32] For totally delicious vegan pancakes – use almond milk and 2 teaspoons of vegetable oil instead of milk, eggs and butter.

INGREDIENTS:

- 100g plain flour
- 1 teaspoon of bicarbonate of soda
- A pinch of fine sea salt
- 150ml buttermilk
- 3 large eggs
- 1 teaspoon of melted butter

RECIPE

1. MIX THE BATTER

Mix everything together (except the butter) using an electric whisk or blender. Don't be tempted to do it by hand – you'll end up with lumps.

2. COOK 'EM

- Heat a large, heavy bottomed frying pan that has been wiped with a smear of butter.
- When it's nice and hot, pour a small ladle of batter into the middle of the pan and cook for 1 minute.
- Flip it over with a spatula and cook for another 60 seconds.
- Keep going until all the batter is used up. You can keep them warm on a plate in a low-heat oven (100°C).

3. SERVE

Stack up your pancakes and drizzle with your favourite topping. For the wow factor use strawberries and chocolate sauce. But remember the nation's favourite topping is good old lemon and sugar! You can make easy chocolate sauce by heating up cream, turning off the heat and then stirring in broken-up bits of chocolate.

WARNING! Yep, you guessed it! If you have allergies, make sure you check the recipe carefully, and always have an adult on hand to help with the cooking.

SECRET NUMBER 58

HOW TO STOP A PAPER CUT HURTING

EVERYBODY THINKS:

Paper cuts are the most annoyingly painful thing ever and there's nothing yo can do about them, just throw a tantrum and scrunch the paper into a little ball and then stamp on it.

BUT SECRET 58 IS THIS:

They don't have to be. Even though paper cuts are probably more painful than having your head chopped off with a guillotine (see **Secret 85: How to blink when you're dead**), that doesn't mean you can't stop them from hurting.

First, let's find out why paper cuts hurt so much:

THREE REASONS PAPER CUTS HURT SO MUCH

REASON 1: There are more pain receptors in your fingertips than almost anywhere else in your body.

REASON 2: When you zoom in, paper is rough like a saw – so it rips, tears, and shreds your nerve endings, rather than making a clean slice.

REASON 3: It cuts *deep enough* to get past the top layer of the skin and expose all the nerve endings. But not so deep that it bleeds a lot to produce a nice, protective scab.

So far, so ouchy. But now you know why, you can stop it hurting fast with a simple trick: a fake scab to protect those exposed nerve endings.

PUT IT TO THE TEST:

Get some Vaseline or lip balm – the waxier the better – and put it on the cut. Once you've sealed it off it should feel a lot better straight away. Keep applying whenever you need to. You're welcome.

HOW TO STOP A MOSQUITO BITE ITCHING

EVERYBODY THINKS:

Mozzie bites are the most annoyingly irritating thing ever. And once you're bitten[33] that's it, you'll be scratching it for days, unable to sleep or ever smile again.

BUT SECRET 59 IS THIS:

If you act fast, you can stop a mosquito bite itching. But you need to act as soon as you notice you're bitten. There are dozens of home remedies for mozzie bites so we put the top three to the test.

PUT IT TO THE TEST:

TOP THREE HOME REMEDIES:

1. **GOLD MEDAL:** Raw honey was the winner, hands down. Leave it on for 30 minutes and job done. But most honey is *pasteurized* (cooked a little) and that *doesn't* work. So, if you don't have any local raw honey, try one of these runners-ups.

2. **SILVER MEDAL:** Bicarbonate of soda needs to be mixed with a little water to make a paste and *then left on overnight.*

3. **BRONZE MEDAL:** Apple cider vinegar works if you mix a tablespoon with a glass of water and then spray it all over your skin. But it's messy and it makes you smell like an old apple.

WARNING! If you have allergies to any of the remedies listed above, don't use them.

---

[33] But if it's not too late, see **Secret 45: How to not be a mosquito magnet**.

HOW TO GROW TALLER

EVERYBODY THINKS:

You can't do anything about your height, it's all in your genes. If you're too tall or too small then blame your parents.

BUT SECRET 60 IS THIS:

Scientists estimate that about 80% of an individual's height is determined by their genes. The remaining 20% is down to four key things: diet, sleep, exercise and posture. These influence how much growth hormone[34] your body produces. Remember, being shorter than average comes with a heap of health benefits and can give you an edge in many sports. But if you want to gain a few extra cm, here's how.

PUT IT TO THE TEST:

First check out **Secret 61: How to find out how tall you'll be when you grow up** and then turbocharge with these top tips:

EAT WELL: Getting plenty of protein is the most important thing. And one type of protein in particular called arginine is important: you can get lots of it from nuts, chicken, fish and eggs. But it's not just about protein – you need to eat a healthy, balanced diet full of vitamins and minerals, so fresh fruit and veg is also really important.

SLEEP: Growth hormone is released at night when you're sleeping. So get a good night's sleep by avoiding screens in the hours before bedtime.[35]
If you're not sure how much sleep you need:

- Children aged 6–13: about 9–12 hours.
- Teenagers aged 14–17: about 8–10 hours.

EXERCISE: Exercise promotes growth hormone production. Get at least one hour of exercise a day.

[34] Growth hormone is a chemical produced in the body that helps control body growth.
[35] For more sleep tips see **Secret 33: How to sleep more**.

SECRET NUMBER 61

HOW TO FIND OUT HOW TALL YOU'LL BE WHEN YOU GROW UP

EVERYBODY THINKS:

You can't predict the future.

BUT SECRET 61 IS THIS:

Height can be predicted with a decent level of accuracy if you have a tape measure and a willing parent (or two) on hand.

PUT IT TO THE TEST:

STEP 1:

Work out the average height of your biological parents.

STEP 2:

Add 7.6cm if you're male. Subtract 7.6cm if you're female. This isn't 100% accurate, but most people will be within 5cm of this (up or down). But, if you eat the right things, sleep and exercise well, you could easily be up to 10cm taller than this. See **Secret 60: How to grow taller** to see if you're doing all the right things.

SECRET NUMBER 62

HOW TO SURVIVE GROUP CHATS

EVERYBODY THINKS:

Group chats are a nightmare. Whether you're on WhatsApp, WeChat, Snapchat or WhateverChat – they're all a total life-sucking, cyberbullying minefield. You'll wake up every day to a million new messages and if you ever do post something yourself, you're bound to upset somebody and they'll hold a grudge for the rest of time.

BUT SECRET 62 IS THIS:

Most online chat *is* group chat. Chat groups can be a really useful way to stay in touch with a whole bunch of people. But group chats can be tricky, even when you know all the people in them. Here are some top tips for keeping stress levels as low as possible:

HOW TO SURVIVE GROUP CHATS:

TURN NOTIFICATIONS OFF: This may be the single most important thing you'll ever do. Turning off all notifications will boost your IQ, make you happier and more successful.[36]

DON'T REPLY IF YOU DON'T NEED TO: Every text doesn't need a "K" from every single person in the group.

SLEEP: There's always someone on a group who texts late at night. Don't be that person.

NEVER ARGUE: No one ever wins an argument in a group chat. You just look like a bully.

EXIT: At times, it can feel like there's no escape from the groups you've found yourself added to. But you can always leave. Don't make a fuss, just bow out gracefully. Trust us, leaving is always better than staying in a group chat that's making you miserable.

---

[36] See also **Secret 41: How to do two things at once**.

STOP CYBERBULLIES: Most cyberbullying happens in group chats. The "Stop, Speak, Support" code is there to help:

1. STOP: When bad banter spoils the party, **STOP**. Instead of ploughing in, stay calm and try to better understand what's going on.

2. SPEAK: Turn to a friend or trusted adult and tell them what's going on.

3. SUPPORT: Support your friends if they're getting flack. Encourage them to talk to someone they trust.

WARNING! Take extra care to keep yourself safe online. My top five safety tips are:

1. NEVER SHARE PERSONAL INFORMATION ONLINE.
2. DON'T RESPOND TO EMAILS, TEXTS OR MESSAGES FROM STRANGERS.
3. DON'T POST OR SHARE PHOTOS ONLINE IN PUBLIC PLACES.
4. DON'T CLICK LINKS, OPEN ATTACHMENTS OR ACCEPT GIFTS FROM SOMEONE YOU DON'T KNOW.
5. NEVER AGREE TO MEET SOMEONE YOU MET ONLINE.

BONUS TIP: For more ways to relax, see **Secret 34: How to get to sleep in two minutes** and **Secret 72: How to look relaxed (when you're not)**.

SECRET NUMBER 63

HOW TO REMEMBER BEING A BABY

EVERYBODY THINKS:

No one can remember being a baby. There's something called "childhood amnesia", which makes it impossible to remember stuff that happened to us when we were really small.

YOUNG LARRY HAYES

BUT SECRET 63 IS THIS:

It is not true that toddlers can't remember much. What is true is that as *adults* we can't retrieve these memories, but as children it's easier. Our first memory tends to be something either really exciting or really horrible. For example, if your parents made you a chocolate hedgehog cake for your 4th birthday – even though you clearly said you didn't like chocolate cake – then you're likely to remember that. BUT, it turns out that we retain "explicit memories" (when we remember an actual event that happened to us) from even younger. You just need to know how to *awaken that trace*.

PUT IT TO THE TEST:

STEP 1: Ask your parent or carer what smells were unique to when you were a baby. Get them to look at some old photos to remind them.

STEP 2: Don't look at the photos yourself! They might give you false memories.

STEP 3: Go for what you liked. Find if there were any particular smells you liked. It might be a specific shampoo or skin cream, or it might be the smell of a plant or food.

STEP 4: Combinations of smells are especially useful. So, if there's a photo of you eating a satsuma in a rose garden … go with that.

STEP 5: Now, close your eyes and try to remember an event from when you were a baby or toddler.

HOW TO BE SARCASTIC AND GET AWAY WITH IT

EVERYBODY THINKS:

Sarcasm is annoying and the lowest form of comedy. Mainly, people use it to say the opposite of what's true to make someone look or feel stupid, and that's just mean.

BUT SECRET 64 IS THIS:

Yeah, right.

... or maybe not. Maybe sarcasm is more useful and funnier than "everybody" thinks.

Sarcasm can be incredibly useful. Just check out these ideas:

GET PARENTS TO STOP ASKING QUESTIONS:

GET YOUR SIBLING TO LEAVE YOU ALONE:

But what about getting away with it? The secret to that is: telling the truth.

WARNING! Being sarcastic too much can be annoying. Save it for special occasions, genius.

SECRET NUMBER 65

HOW TO WIN LOADS OF STUFF

EVERYBODY THINKS:

Winning stuff is down to chance or being brilliant. Everybody also says, "You have to be in it, to win it." Which is just a really pointlessly obvious thing to say.

BUT SECRET 65 IS THIS:

If you fancy a holiday in the Maldives, a new computer or £500 in sweets – then read on. Competition experts (known as "compers") claim you can win prizes worth £££ every year by entering free competitions.

You just need to know a few comping tips and tricks.

PUT IT TO THE TEST:

FIVE TRICKS TO COMPING SUCCESS

TIP 1: GO FREE

Only ever enter free competitions.

TIP 2: BE PICKY

Only ever enter "slogan" or "tie-breaker" competitions which have a "25 words or les type requirement. Use a search engine to find them.

TIP 3: BE CAREFUL

Use an adult's standalone email to avoid spam (with their permission!).

TIP 4: BE WITTY & CLEVER

OK, this is the tricky part, but it's not as hard as most people think. Write down every word you can think of relating to the question and the product and then write somethi either funny, awe-inspiring, clever or that rhymes. If in doubt, cheat for ideas.

TIP 5: CHECK IT

Make sure you haven't gone over the word count!

> **WARNING!** Something can be free in terms of money, but involve you selling your data and sometimes personal data to third parties...

HOW TO LET PEOPLE KNOW YOU'RE AWESOME

EVERYBODY THINKS:

You're either awesome or you're not. And most of us are not.

BUT SECRET 66 IS THIS:

You don't need to be rated by others as "awesome". You know that you are awesome. So, if you want people to know how awesome you are, try focusing on one of these six habits each day for a whole week. You should notice fewer arguments, and happier friends. Awesome!

HABIT 1: POSITIVE AND NEGATIVE EMPATHY

They can put themselves in someone else's shoes and genuinely feel what they are feeling – either good or bad.

HABIT 2: BEING HUMBLE

People who are genuinely enjoyable to be around are humble, not boasty.

HABIT 3: HAVING A SENSE OF HUMOUR

This is the number one thing that sets popular people apart. Research shows that when it comes to how we rate people socially, a sense of humour is more important than looks, intelligence and sporting ability all put together!

HABIT 4: BE GENUINELY INTERESTED IN EVERYONE

Guess what the favourite topic of conversation for most people is? Themselves. Do the opposite and you'll become super popular, very quickly.

HABIT 5: GOSSIP POSITIVELY

Say nice things about other people behind their back, and you'll see your social status soar.

HABIT 6: ASK FOR ADVICE

Asking for advice makes people think you're smart and confident. It also sends them the message that you like them and respect their opinion.

SECRET NUMBER 67

HOW TO SURVIVE BEING STRUCK BY LIGHTNING

EVERYBODY THINKS:

The chances of being struck by lightning are tiny. But if you do get hit, you're a goner.

BUT SECRET 67 IS THIS:

Actually, you're much more likely to get struck by lightning than win the Lotto Jackpot. Even so, your best bet is to avoid being struck in the first place.

HOW TO AVOID BEING STRUCK BY LIGHTNING:

THE 30/30 RULE

If there's less than 30 seconds between thunder and lightning then it's time to get to safety. Wait for 30 minutes after the last thunderclap before going back out.[37]

WHEN THUNDER ROARS, GO INDOORS

Your ideal shelter is a large, enclosed building or car (avoid touching glass or metal).

Keep away from water, high places, large open spaces and tall isolated objects (like trees).

But if you *can't* avoid lightning, you can still survive. Lightning can hit the ground first and then go up into your body, so crouch on the balls of your feet to reduce the risk. If you touch your heels together, if lighting comes up one foot, it's likely to go down the other.

WARNING! Remember, when thunder roars, stay indoors and always keep away from lightning.

---

[37] Count the seconds between lightning and thunderclap then divide by three to give you the distance in kilometres. So, if there's a 30 second gap, the lightning is 10 km away.

HOW TO STOP A NOSEBLEED

EVERYBODY THINKS:

You tip your head back and pinch your nose to stop a nosebleed.

BUT SECRET 68 IS THIS:

You tip your head forward not back.
Here's the full guide:

HOW TO STOP A NOSEBLEED:

STEP 1: Sit down at a table and lean forward. Breathe through your mouth – spit out any blood that collects in your throat or mouth into a bowl; do not swallow any blood.

STEP 2: Firmly pinch the soft part of your nose, just above your nostrils.

STEP 3: Place an ice pack or bag of frozen vegetables covered by a towel on your forehead or back of your neck.

STEP 4: Stay upright or seated, rather than lying down, as this reduces the blood pressure in the blood vessels of your nose and will help reduce further bleeding.

Most nosebleeds stop within 5–10 minutes. They usually don't cause enough blood loss to be serious.

PUT IT TO THE TEST:

No, if you do the following you won't have to: keep your nails short, pick your nose less and avoid really dry air.

WARNING! Go to A&E if:

- Your nosebleed lasts longer than 15 minutes.
- The bleeding seems excessive.
- You're swallowing a large amount of blood.
- The bleeding started after a serious injury.

And remember, always tell a parent or teacher if you are having a nosebleed, so that they can make sure you are OK!

SECRET NUMBER (69)

HOW TO MAKE SOMEONE ADMIT THEY'RE LYING

EVERYBODY THINKS:

You need to be a Jedi or an interrogation expert to get someone to admit when they're lying.

BUT SECRET 69 IS THIS:

The American CIA spy agency has some fool-proof techniques for getting people to spill the beans and anyone can learn them. They rely on three things: being friendly, understanding and cunning.

PUT IT TO THE TEST:

DON'T:

DO IT IN FRONT OF OTHER PEOPLE
Nobody confesses to a crowd.

GET ANGRY
They'll just clam up.

USE ACCUSING QUESTIONS
It suggests you're not sure.

DO:

GO ALONE AND BRING FOOD

People are more open and trusting when they're eating.

SHOW SOME LOVE AND NOD YOUR HEAD

Research shows that people talk three times more if the listener nods their head.

USE QUESTIONS THAT PRESUME THEY DID IT

It shows you know the truth.

HOW TO WORK LESS (AND ACHIEVE MORE)

EVERYBODY THINKS:

You can't achieve success without hard work. In fact, they're so convinced that just about every successful person has made a clever quote about working hard – from Albert Einstein to Yoda.

BUT SECRET 70 IS THIS:

Sometimes less is more. In fact, studies show that the perfect number of hours to work each day is five. And with a few tips we can do more in three hours than most people do in a full eight-hour workday. That means you'll free up time for all the fun stuff in life: play more video games, go surfing, scuba diving. Anything! Here's how.

WORK LESS – ACHIEVE MORE

HYPERFOCUS: Cut out all distractions. Put your phone in a different room, turn off all notifications and never, ever, try to do two things at once (and don't read **Secret 41: How to do two things at once** – rip the pages out now and stamp on them). If you find yourself daydreaming, listen to instrumental music.

WORK IN BURSTS: Research shows that the most productive people work in 52-minute bursts then take a 17-minute break of total rest, play and fun. So set an alarm and make sure you stop when the 52 minutes is up.

PARKINSON'S LAW: This law states that "The more time you have to do a job, the longer it takes." So set yourself a hard deadline.[38]

[38] See also **Secret 38: How to tidy faster**.

FIND YOUR 20%: Look at all the work you do and find the 20% that's the most productive. Then just do that. So, if the best way to learn maths for an exam is to do practice questions in an app … just do practice questions in an app.[39]

LOOK AFTER NUMBER ONE: *You* are number one – make sure you get plenty of sleep, eat well, see friends and family and get outdoors. Time spent doing all that can double what you can get done.

PUT IT TO THE TEST:

---

[39] See also **Secret 47: How to pass exams without working up a sweat**.

SECRET NUMBER 71

HOW TO LEARN A FOREIGN LANGUAGE IN SEVEN WEEKS

EVERYBODY THINKS:

You can't learn a language in seven weeks. It's more like seven years.

BUT SECRET 71 IS THIS:

It is possible to learn a language in seven weeks, but you need to be young, motivated and spend at least 30 minutes a day studying. The *best* age to learn a new language is under ten years of age. But don't worry if you're older, as long as you're under 17, you should be fine. Oldies will just need to put in a lot more effort.

The best way to learn is naturally, by living with people who speak the language. So if you're suddenly plonked into a foreign school, don't panic, you'll naturally be able to communicate pretty well after seven weeks.

The second-best way is to use a language app and know a few tricks to super-boost your learning. 30 minutes a day for seven weeks[40] on a free language learning app will get you to about 2,000 words and able to communicate in most everyday situations. You won't be completely fluent, but you will get to GCSE level.

PUT IT TO THE TEST:

Download a language app. Use it for 30 minutes a day and aim for a 42-day streak. Then use these six tricks to super-boost your learning.

---

[40] If you can't manage 30 minutes a day, 15 minutes a day for 14 weeks is just as good!

LANGUAGE SUPER-BOOST TIPS

TIP 1: SET YOURSELF A REWARD

At the end of the 42-day streak. Maybe persuade a parent or grandparent to reward you with something BIG.

TIP 2: LEARN AN EASY "CATEGORY 1" LANGUAGE

Like French, Italian, Spanish or Portuguese. Category 4 languages like Japanese or Mandarin take four times as long to learn. Toki Pona is arguably the fastest to learn in the world, with only 120 words.[41]

TIP 3: KEEP TALKING

When you're using an app, say things out loud all the time – especially new words. Say them at least *twice each time*. This is the most important tip: doing it will *help you learn 50% faster.*

TIP 4: LISTEN TO MUSIC AND WATCH CARTOONS

Listen to music in the language you're learning and watch kids' cartoons. Don't worry about understanding everything, just listening to the language while chilling out will help enormously.

TIP 5: LEARN IN YOUR SLEEP

Listening to foreign language podcasts when you're falling asleep won't help you learn new words, but it will solidify what you've already learned.

TIP 6: GET TO THE MAGIC LEVEL

So you never forget what you've learned. The magic level is the point where you know a language well enough that it's *useful*. You might be able to watch a movie in that language or read simple books or comics. Once you can do that, you'll most likely remember it for ever.

---

[41] Even easier is to make up your own language. See *How to Be a Kid Boss*, **Secret 57: How to make up your own secret language**.

SECRET NUMBER 72

HOW TO LOOK RELAXED (WHEN YOU'RE NOT)

EVERYBODY THINKS:

It's totally obvious when someone is stressed. They blush, shake, sweat, bite their nails and go boggle-eyed. This is a real problem if you're a nervous surgeon.

BUT SECRET 72 IS THIS:

It's OK being nervous, but sometimes you might want to hide it. And the good news is that here are seven hacks to instantly look more confident. And best of all, they'll even make you feel more confident.

CONFIDENCE HACKS

1. STAND TALL
With your head high.

2. DO SOME MATHS
To change your brain activity.

3. KEEP YOUR HANDS STILL
By holding them together.

4. DO THE "MAGIC DOUBLE BREATH"
(See **Secret 25: How to not blush**).

5. POWER STANCE
Stand wit legs apar

6. FAKE EYE CONTACT
By looking other people eyebrows.

7. CHEW GUM
For instant stress relief.

ECRET NUMBER 73

HOW TO TICKLE YOURSELF

EVERYBODY THINKS:

Tickling yourself is impossible. Try it: it just doesn't work. It's one of the three great mysteries of the universe.[42]

BUT SECRET 73 IS THIS:

The answer lies in the back of your brain in a bit called the cerebellum. It monitors your movements and so your brain knows exactly what sensation to expect – and so cancels out its response to the tickle.

There are ways to get round this. If there's a time delay between your hand moving and the tickle, then your cerebellum gets confused. So, if you can build a time delay robot that delays your self-tickle by about a fifth of a second, then you'll be able to tickle yourself.

BUT, who's got the time to build a time delay robot? Go for the easy method instead:

PUT IT TO THE TEST?

This is no laughing matter – do this and you could become the second person in the world to tickle themselves without using a robot. Good luck:

THE EASY METHOD

STEP 1: Get a stick, lots of feathers, elastic bands and paper clips.

STEP 2: Use the paper clips and elastic bands to make a multijointed tickle stick, a bit like this one:

STEP 3: Tickle yourself! All those joints in the tickle stick cause a time delay and some randomness in the feather movement.

---

[42] The other two are: Why do your fingers go shrivelly in the bath? And how come some kids get sweets for breakfast?

SECRET NUMBER 74

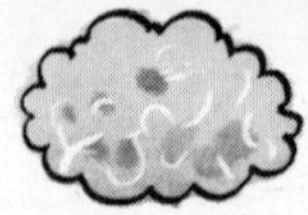

HOW TO SURVIVE A ZOMBIE APOCALYPSE

EVERYBODY THINKS:

They know how to survive a zombie apocalypse. That's what all those movies and video games are for: training.

BUT SECRET 74 IS THIS:

The movies have got it wrong; in real life, zombies would be very different.

ZOMBIE FACTS VS FICTION

IN MOVIES:	IN REAL LIFE:
THE INFECTION HITS HUMANS FIRST.	**UNLIKELY!** Infection is likely to cross over from another species like bats, pigs or chickens.
AN INFECTION CHANGES PEOPLE'S BRAINS.	**TRUE!** Many infections change the way your brain works. Rabies is most the famous example but there's also toxo, commonly found in cat poo, that makes people more outgoing and impulsive.
THE ZOMBIE DISEASE QUICKLY SPREADS ACROSS THE WHOLE PLANET.	**POSSIBLE!** Pandemics can spread around the world, thanks to aeroplane travel.
ZOMBIES ARE HARD TO KILL.	**FALSE!** Zombies would have a working heart and blood system, so even though they don't feel pain, you can inflict fatal damage on the undead.

ZOMBIES WALK FUNNY.	**LIKELY!** An infection which changes your brain so much that you lose consciousness is likely to affect your "cerebellum" – the bit of your brain used for fine motor function.
ZOMBIES LIVE ON HUMAN FLESH.	**UNLIKELY!** Zombies are likely to need water just like everybody else. Cut off their water supply and they'll die out in about three days.
ZOMBIES TAKE OVER THE WORLD.	**UNLIKELY!** Zombies will quickly die out because they're less brainy and able to survive than humans.

PUT IT TO THE TEST:

You'll be disappointed to learn that the chances of getting some real-life zombie action are approximately 0%. But just in case, here are five top tips:

TOP TIP 1: LIVE IN NEW ZEALAND

Or somewhere remote. Zombies will be rubbish at travelling/flying planes.

TOP TIP 2: OR LIVE IN A HOSPITAL

They have back-up generators for power and lots of medical equipment and staff.[43]

TOP TIP 3: HAVE A DIESEL CAR

For emergency escape and for foraging.

TOP TIP 4: GET A WATER FILTER

This is the #1 bit of equipment you need. In a zombie apocalypse, thirst would be the biggest killer.

TOP TIP 5: PREP YOUR SURVIVAL KIT

It should include soap, duct tape, wind-up radio, multi-vitamins and spare pants.

---

[43] Best of all, live in a remote hospital in New Zealand.

SECRET NUMBER 75

HOW TO BE CLEVERER THAN A TEENAGER

EVERYBODY THINKS:

Teenagers are cleverer than younger kids because they're older and can do GCSEs and stuff.

THINGS TEENAGERS ARE GENIUSES AT:

1. LOOKING BORED
2. SLEEPING
3. MAKING ADULTS FEEL OLD

BUT SECRET 75 IS THIS:

Teenagers are cleverer at some things, but not everything. Teenagers actually lose connections between brain cells in a process called "pruning". The connections left are stronger and more efficient but in the short term, while all the pruning is going on, they're weaker. This pruning process starts at the back of the brain and works to the front.

The occipital lobe at the back is responsible for processing vision, so teenagers are actually worse at, say, recognizing people's faces than younger kids. It also prunes away some memories. So, all that French you learned in primary school? Keep using it, or you'll lose it.

Finally, the pruning remodels the prefrontal cortex at the front. The prefrontal cortex is the decision-making part at the front of the brain. It's responsible for planning and thinking about the consequences of actions, solving problems and controlling impulses. So, teens are more impulsive and risk-taking. They also feel more and have stronger emotions.

So, if you've got an older sibling, remind them that their brain might not be as good as yours. And if you're a teen already, then remember that being clumsy, forgetting stuff, doing stupid stuff and eating loads of doughnuts is normal. And it won't last for ever, so cut yourself some slack. The best you can do is to be good to your developing brain – because what you do as a teen will change your brain for life. Get plenty of sleep, exercise and eat decent food and keep screen time down. But also, remind your parents that no one died of an untidy bedroom.

PUT IT TO THE TEST:

The average pre-teen will do this test better than the average teenager. See how long it takes to spot the odd one out.

KEY:
< 20 SECONDS = KID GENIUS
20–40 SECONDS = AVERAGE ADULT
> 40 SECONDS = TEENAGER
> 1 HOUR = YOUR EYES ARE SHUT

SECRET NUMBER 76

HOW TO FIND OUT WHAT HAPPENS WHEN WE DIE

EVERYBODY THINKS:

The only way to find out what happens when you're dead, is when you're dead. So, ask a dead person.

BUT SECRET 76 IS THIS:

Every year, thousands of people have a Near Death Experience (or NDE). They report that it doesn't feel like a dream or a hallucination and often say the experience was "more real than real life". NDEs often share six remarkable features.

SIX FEATURES OF AN NDE:

1. Starts with the sensation of floating up and seeing yourself.
2. Spending time in a beautiful, otherworldly realm.
3. Meeting spiritual beings.
4. And a loving presence.
5. Encountering long-lost relatives or friends.
6. A sensation of being drawn into a tunnel or darkness.

HOW TO SLOW DOWN YOUR HEART RATE LIKE A NINJA

EVERYBODY THINKS:

The whole ninja thing is mainly made up. They couldn't really do all that *Ninja Focus* stuff, and Teenage Mutant Ninja Turtles are definitely not real.

BUT SECRET 77 IS THIS:

For over 500 years Ninja, or more accurately Shinobi, have trained to be secret warriors and spies with seemingly superhuman powers. Shinobi literally translates as "Those who act in stealth" and they learn a very specific martial art: Ninjitsu. There's also a technique for slowing down you heart rate in order to hide undetected for long periods. It essentially involves "The Art of No Mind" … emptying your mind of all thought.

Now for most people, that can take years of meditation and practice, so we've applied some modern science to come up with a short cut. Even if you're not planning on becoming a secret assassin or secret agent, it's incredibly useful for dealing with stressful situations.

PUT IT TO THE TEST:

1. LET YOUR BRAIN DO ITS THING: Don't try to empty your mind, instead let a thought come and then practise letting it go, ready for the next thought to pop up. Sooner or later, your brain will run out of things to think about.

2. BREATHE OUT: All the time you're breathing out, your heart rate gets slower. When you're breathing in, it's getting faster. So just make sure you breathe out slowly and your heart rate will drop.

WARNING! While it's great to feel calm, normal breathing is good too, so only use this technique when you need to.

SECRET NUMBER 78

HOW TO COME BACK FROM THE DEAD

EVERYBODY THINKS:

The only certainty in life is death. You can't come back from the dead unless you're a zombie[44] or an immortal jellyfish. We know this because if someone did come back from being dead, they would go on about it *a lot*.

BUT SECRET 78 IS THIS:

Things come back from the dead all the time – and not just immortal jellyfish. Some bacteria can be brought back from death with just a little bit of nitrogen gas. And if a flatworm gets cut in half, it can grow into *two* flatworms.

And then there's the tardigrade, or "water bear", the most indestructible species on the planet. They live on mossy trees all over the planet and when life gets tough, they curl up and die. But tardigrades are tougher than you think:

TARDIGRADES ARE TOUGH

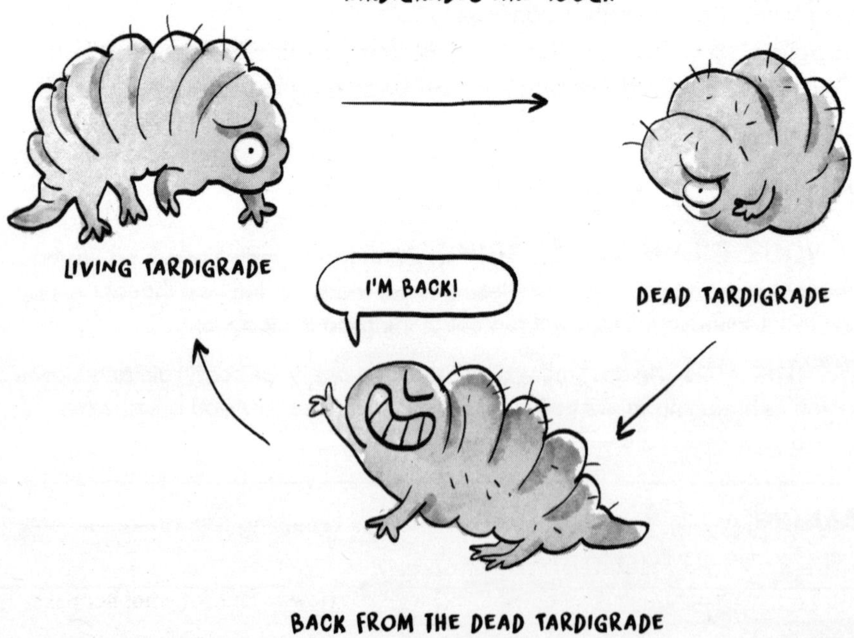

But what if you're not a tardigrade? What about humans? Well, a common question for paramedics is, "Is it possible to bring people back from the dead?" and the answer might surprise you. It's yes.

But there's a catch: you can't be too dead. When breathing and blood flow stop, scientists believe there's a window of about four minutes before brain damage kicks in. After that comes biological death, or brain death, and there's no turning back from that.[45]

But what if we could extend that four-minute window? Many scientists believe it's possible to do so by freezing the brain to keep it fresh. If it can work for a fishfinger, why not a brain?

Experiments with 40,000-year-old worms dug out of the permafrost in Siberia show that – if you warm up the worms very, very slowly – their brains work just fine. And all over the world there are companies offering to freeze you when you die ready to be brought back to life in the future when doctors have figured out how to do it. Human immortality is available for the low, low price of £40 a month!

PUT IT TO THE TEST:

We suggest that you don't put you sibling in the freezer until scientists have figured out how to bring them back to life. But if you do want to bring something back from the dead, here's how.

Freeze some live yoghurt in the freezer (the bacteria can be brought back to life after two months in the freezer). Then, when you next fancy some yoghurt, defrost it and eat it up! Bonus: it is so healthy; you'll probably live for ever.

---

[44] But see **Secret 74: How to survive a zombie apocalypse**.

[45] But read about "Near Death Experiences" in **Secret 76: How to find out what happens when we die**.

SECRET NUMBER 79

HOW TO NOT WEE YOURSELF WHEN YOU'RE TERRIFIED

EVERYBODY THINKS:

They won't really wee themselves if they get scared. Surely?

BUT SECRET 79 IS THIS:

Most animals wee when they're frightened – from pigeons to porcupines. And humans are no different. Your brain controls your bladder in a complicated way. There are three systems at work:

1. BASIC PONS SYSTEM

When your bladder's full, the nerves in the bladder send a signal to a bit of your brainstem called the pons that tells the sphincter muscle to relax and empty your bladder. This is the same system reptiles and mice have and it's why they wee all the time.

2. ADVANCED CORTEX SYSTEM

Luckily, humans are more advanced than lizards and mice. We have an extra brain system that can override the pons and tell it to wait. It's in the cortex, the advanced outer layer of our brains where all the grey cells live.

3. FIGHT–OR–FLIGHT SYSTEM

When you have a fright – say you're being chased by a clown through a haunted house – then a bit of your brain called the limbic system gets your body ready to either fight or run fast. It floods your system with stress hormones and it can also stop the brain signal from the cortex to the pons – causing you to wee.

That's all very well but it still doesn't answer the question of how you stop it happening!

Well, the first thing to remember is that it happens to most people if they're scared enough. And it can happen to *anyone*, even special forces combat troops. So don't sweat it. But if you do want some tips, check out these military training tricks:

PUT IT TO THE TEST:

FOUR MILITARY TRICKS TO CONQUER FEAR:

TIP 1: PRACTISE Put yourself in situations similar to those you're worried about.

TIP 2: BE THE JOKER Practise laughing or coming up with jokes in the face of scary things.

TIP 3: BREATHE Slow it down and breathe in for four seconds, then out for four seconds.

TIP 4: DON'T BOTTLE IT UP If you're scared of something, admitting it to family or friends is the best thing for you. Hearing yourself say stuff out loud helps you put it out in the open and confront it head on.

SECRET NUMBER 80

HOW TO TELL IF YOUR CRUSH LIKES YOU BACK

EVERYBODY THINKS:

Love is an enigma wrapped in a riddle buried under a mountain of confusion. There's no way of knowing if your crush likes you back.

BUT SECRET 80 IS THIS:

With a few psychology top tips, you can become a mind-reader. To begin with, learn to read body language from **Secret 4: How to tell what someone is *really* thinking**. But body language is just one way of discovering the truth. There are three others: what they talk about, how they behave socially and how they communicate digitally.

PUT IT TO THE TEST:

Ask yourself the 12 questions on the next page and if you get yes to at least half ... there's a really good chance they like you back.[46] You're ready for **Secret 82: How to ask someone out**. Good luck.

[46] But remember, even with this test, your crush might just want to be friends. Try not to take rejection as a reflection on yourself (you're awesome) and make sure not to accuse them of leading you on – they may be completely unaware of how you feel.

BODY LANGUAGE

1. Nervy – Are they anxious or hyper around you?
2. Eyes – Are their pupils dilated (bigger) when they look at you?
3. Feet – Are they pointing towards you?
4. Lean – Do they lean towards you when you're talking?

MEANINGFUL CONVERSATIONS

5. Do they ask lots of questions about you?
6. Do they tell you things they don't tell others?

SOCIAL BEHAVIOUR

7. Do they laugh at your jokes?
8. Do they laugh at your jokes even when they're not funny?
9. Do they smarten themselves up for you?
10. Do they become more playful or show off more when you're there?

DIGITAL COMMS

11. Do they react a lot on social media?
12. Do they text you at all different times of day (and not just in the evening when they're bored)?

CRET NUMBER 81

HOW TO CHANGE YOUR NAME

EVERYBODY THINKS:

If you're called Colin, sorry, but you're stuck with it.

BUT SECRET 81 IS THIS:

If you're over 16, you can change your name using a short legal document called a deed poll. You just need to print it off and sign it in front of two witnesses. Then *BAM!* You've got a new name.

PUT IT TO THE TEST:

Probs best not to, eh? Being called "I Am Cheese" is only funny for so long...

SECRET NUMBER 82

HOW TO ASK SOMEONE OUT

EVERYBODY THINKS:

It's impossible asking someone out, even adults can't do it. It's actually easier and safer kissing a hungry piranha than asking someone out face-to-face. The worst thing that can happen is the piranha eats your face off. Whereas … asking someone out risks the horror of lifelong humiliation and misery.

BUT SECRET 82 IS THIS:

You can do this: with a few tips, it doesn't need to be impossible. Just follow these simple Dos and Don't.

DO:

BE FRIENDS
First hang out together, spend some time in a group setting, ask open meaningful questions and be friendly. (Don't worry it's all in **Secret 11: How to make a friend for life.**)

FIND OUT IF THEY LIKE YOU BACK
Read **Secret 80: How to tell if your crush likes you back**, to get some tips.

PICK THE RIGHT TIME
When they're not stressed or sad or surrounded by millions of people.

USE A CONFIDENCE BOOSTER
Such as the Magic Double Breath to get yourself calm, and use the Eye Contact Trick if you're still struggling (read about both in **Secret 25: How to not blush**).

SMALL TALK FIRST
Don't just blurt it out.

BE SPECIFIC
Think of a thing you could do together and ask them to do that specific thing.

DON'T:

ASK SOMEONE OUT WHO YOU DON'T REALLY KNOW.

RUSH IN
If you're not sure they like you give it a few weeks.

GO BIG
Avoid banners flying behind light aircraft, and don't be tempted to do it in the dinner hall at lunch time. Leave the outlandish public appeals of love to romantic movies.

DO IT WITH A NOTE
A text is even worse.

ASK THEM TO BE YOUR GIRLFRIEND/BOYFRIEND
Until you've spent more time together.

TAKE IT BADLY IF THEY SAY NO
Remember, your crush may not be aware of your feelings.

PUT IT TO THE TEST:

Or don't, you can always wait and see if they ask you first. Just keep having fun hanging out with them and see what happens. And there's always the CHEAT CODE.

> **CHEAT CODE:** There's a cheat that's as old as human civilization. If this all seems way too hard you can always ask a friend to let your crush know you like them.

HOW TO WIN A STARE-OFF

EVERYBODY THINKS:

Being good at staring isn't an important life skill. So don't worry about it.

BUT SECRET 83 IS THIS:

That's rubbish – being able to outstare somebody is a really useful life skill. People tend to like and trust others with appropriate eye contact (defined as eye contact for just over half the time you're talking). But if you're rubbish at keeping eye contact, don't worry, playing staring contests are great practice and will make it easier. And with a few top tips, you'll never lose a stare-off again.

PUT IT TO THE TEST:

Not everyone loves a stare-off, so make sure you check that your opponent is game before you play. The rules are simple: you lose if you blink, laugh or look away.

1. Practise in the mirror.
2. Close your eyes tightly right before the contest begins.
3. Squint slightly every so often.
4. If you can, yawn to produce a few tears.
5. Or think of something that makes you angry or sad to release tears.
6. If you're getting desperate – cross your eyes – it might make them laugh.

CRET NUMBER 84

HOW TO GET BOGEYS THAT GLOW IN THE DARK

EVERYBODY THINKS:

Glow in the dark bogeys would be really fun – but no, it'll never happen.

BUT SECRET 84 IS THIS:

Creatures have evolved to create light using the energy released from chemical reactions in order to give themselves a survival advantage. Different creatures put the light to different uses:

DEFENCE: Toxic fish, shrimp and worms scare predators through sudden bursts of light.

ATTACK: Angler fish lure prey with their light.

COMMUNICATION: Fireflies attract a mate using bioluminescence.

ENTERTAINMENT: Humans entertain friends with glow-in-the-dark bogeys.

Unfortunately, that last one isn't true.

But don't give up. Because the real **Secret 84** is that *all bogeys glow in the dark*.

PUT IT TO THE TEST:

HOW TO SEE YOUR GLOW-IN-THE-DARK BOGEY:

STEP 1: You'll need a big bogey, a shoebox and a phone camera with night mode.

STEP 2: Put the bogey and the camera in the shoe box and seal it shut so no light can get in. Make sure the camera is on night mode and that you've set up voice activation so you can tell it to take a photo (use an app if it's not built-in).

STEP 3: Tell the remote control take a photo of the bogey.

STEP 4: Admire your bogey. You should see a faint glow.

SECRET NUMBER (85)

HOW TO BLINK WHEN YOU'RE DEAD

EVERYBODY THINKS:

It's impossible to do anything when you're dead. And besides, what would be the point? You're dead.

BUT SECRET 85 IS THIS:

Doing anything when you're dead has to be the number one, best way of freaking people out. Who wouldn't want to do that? Plus, it's really easy – a proven by dedicated scientist Antoine Lavoisier.

Antoine was such a great scientist that when he was sentenced to beheading during the French Revolution, he grabbed the chance to carry ou one last experiment. This is what Lavoisier's scientific notes may have looke like (you'll notice that the "results" section is in different handwriting).

Blinking After Death

Hypothesis: *A human can carry on blinking after their head's been chopped off.*

Method: *Get arrested, have head chopped off by a guillotine, try to carry on blinking.*

Results: The head blinked for thirty seconds after it had been chopped off. Well done Antoine, you were right!

BONUS FACT: Lavoisier was pardoned a year after his beheading. So as the French say, "Tout est bien qui finit bien".[47]

[47] "All's well that ends well".

BONUS BONUS FACT: If you think Lavoisier was impressive – you should meet Mike the Headless Chicken who lived for 18 months after his head had been cut off. After the loss of his head, Mike achieved national fame until his death in March 1947. The explanation was that although most of his head was severed, most of his brain stem (the lower bit of brain at the top of the spinal cord) was left on his body. Basic functions (like breathing and heart rate) as well as most of a chicken's reflex actions are controlled by the brain stem, so Mike was able to remain quite healthy.

PUT IT TO THE TEST:

We don't recommend it, but maybe you could: build a time machine, go back to post-revolutionary France, become an aristocrat, get arrested and remember to blink loads while you're waiting for the guillotine to drop. Or, if you want to see what cool reflex actions humans do have that are controlled by your brainstem, try this:

BRAIN STEM REFLEX TEST

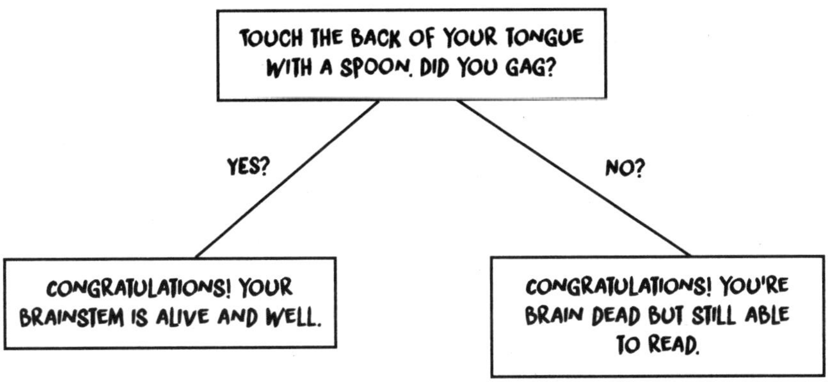

WARNING! Don't put the spoon too far down your throat and, if you start gagging, take the spoon out straight away!

BONUS FACT: Having your head chopped off by a guillotine is probably less painful than a paper cut. see **Secret 58: How to stop a paper cut hurting**.

SECRET NUMBER 86

HOW TO BREATHE UNDERWATER

EVERYBODY THINKS:

Breathing underwater is called, "drowning" and it's really bad for you.

BUT SECRET 86 IS THIS:

Although breathing underwater is always totally fatal for humans, in the future it might not be. Russian scientists have developed a liquid breathing technology which involves breathing in a liquid that's super-rich in oxygen. It has been tested for up to half an hour and as deep as 500 metres "without any health consequences".

It's thought that this sort of technology could help us travel long distances in space and also help babies who were born too early.

PUT IT TO THE TEST:

Uh, let's sit this one out. Any attempt to breathe underwater without the special formula will result in death.

HOW TO TALK TO AN ALIEN

EVERYBODY THINKS:

Aliens look a bit like us but with a big head, long arms and legs, big buggy eyes and funny colour. Everybody also thinks they will have mouths, ears and advanced tech so they can speak our language.

BUT SECRET 87 IS THIS:

If there is alien life out there, it's more likely to look like slime than something more complex because the chances of evolving into multi-celled organisms are tiny. So good luck talking to that.

But there's a twist. Ever since the first radio signal was sent by Marconi in 1893 radio waves have been travelling into space *at the speed of light*. Our broadcasts have now reached over 130 light years from Earth (and over 2,000 Earth-sized planets!).

PUT IT TO THE TEST:

So, if you can't be bothered to go alien hunting, there is an easier way to talk to aliens. Just get yourself on the radio or TV and send them a message that way. Maybe do a phone-in?

The signal will partly leak out into space and by the time you're 26,000 years old, it will have reached the edge of the galaxy. Not bad for a phone-in! Just think carefully what you're going to say – you never know who (or what) will be listening.

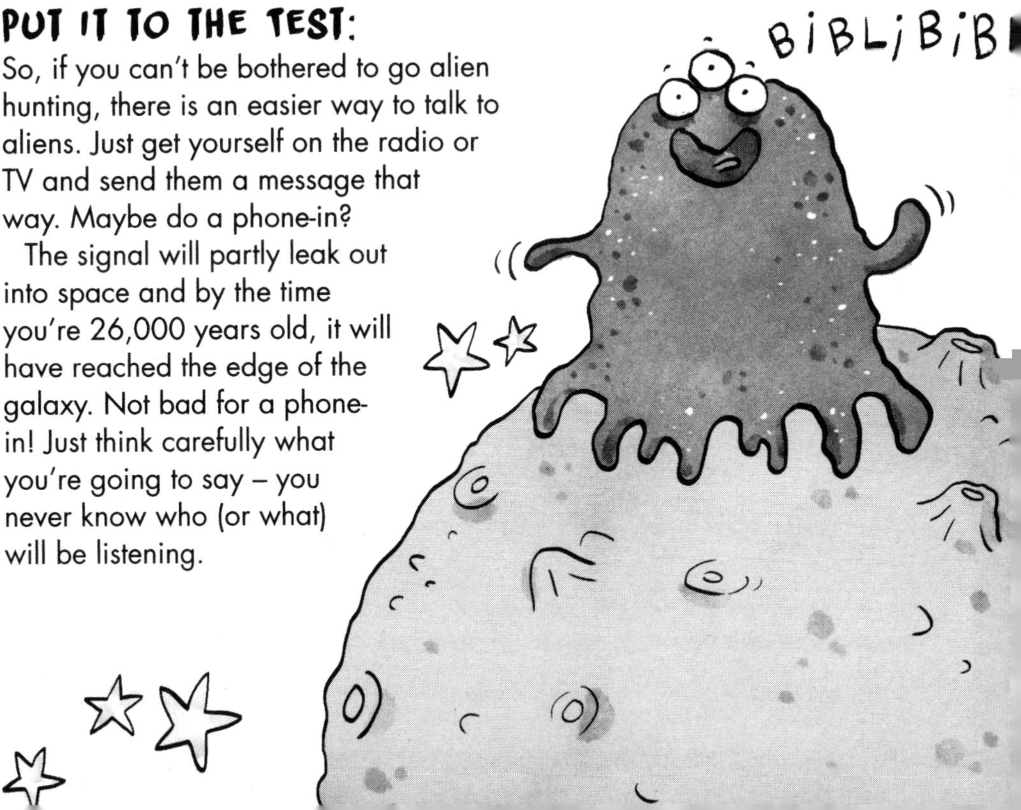

SECRET NUMBER 88

HOW TO SEE A UFO

EVERYBODY THINKS:

UFOs are all made up and if they're not, it's probably under military protection and all very hush-hush. The universe is huge, so why would an alien come all the way here to fly around and not actually say hello?

BUT SECRET 88 IS THIS:

UFOs are real! Flying objects that no one can identify are seen all the time. That doesn't mean they're aliens. It just means there's a mystery to be solved – one way or another. Let's start with what we do know…

SIX WEIRD UFO FACTS:

1. The US government receives about 100 UFO reports a month.
2. A large number of UFOs are reported near nuclear power stations.
3. UFOs are seen all over the world – even by scientists in Antarctica!
4. More UFOs are reported in France and the USA than in any other country.
5. The most common shapes are saucers, cigars and black triangles.
6. Even the ancient Romans and Vikings reported UFOs.

But where do you even start looking for a UFO? And what are you looking for? We've put together a beginner's guide.

PUT IT TO THE TEST:

UFO SPOTTING GUIDE

1. WHERE TO LOOK

San Clemente, Chile, is the UFO capital of the world. UFOs are spotted there most weeks. But most countries have a UFO hotspot. In the UK it's near Stonehenge, Wiltshire. The North Yorkshire moors are also top notch.

2. THINGS MOST OFTEN MISTAKEN FOR UFOS

Steady moving lights, flashing each second = an aircraft.

Steady moving light high in sky with no flashing = a satellite.

Orange flickering light, floating about 50 metres above the ground = a paper lantern.

A very bright point of light in the sky that lasts momentarily, then disappears again = a low-orbit satellite.

A fast-moving, bright object which may travel a large distance across the sky in a split second = a meteorite.

A bright light bulb shape on the ceiling = a lightbulb.

3. HOW TO REPORT IT

If what you see doesn't match any of the above then you may have a true UFO on your hands. Rapidly moving objects which change direction are particularly hard to explain. Get a video or photo if you can, write down what you saw, and note the exact time and location. Every country has its own UFO reporting systems. In the UK, send it to the

BRITISH UFO RESEARCH ASSOCIATION.

SECRET NUMBER (89)

HOW TO PREDICT THE FUTURE WITH DREAMS

EVERYBODY THINKS:

Dreams are just brain farts we have when we're asleep. Even though we spend about two hours a night dreaming, each one's a total mystery and we have no idea what's going on. And they certainly can't predict the future.

BUT SECRET 89 IS THIS:

Neuroscientists have discovered loads about dreams. For one thing, about one in every three people believe they've had a dream that predicted the future. But to understand why so many people think dreams can predict the future, we need to understand *why we dream.*

Dreams, it turns out, have lots of different uses:

WHY WE DREAM

1. **REDUCE ANXIETY:** Dreams allow us to relive memories and experience future worries in the absence of a key stress chemical. That lets our brains experience things in a calmer, safer environment.

2. **BUILD MEMORY:** They help shift memories from short-term to long-term storage in your brain. So if you stop someone whose dreaming they'll struggle to remember stuff they've learnt that day.

3. **SOLVE PROBLEMS:** By testing out past and future events that are worrying us – *dreams help us to test out lots of different solutions.*

So, the secret is – some of the time – our dreams are trying to solve future problems, or experience future stressful events. In other words, when we dream, our brains are often *trying to imagine the future*. When they predict wrongly, we call them nonsense dreams. When they predict correctly – we think they've predicted the future!

PUT IT TO THE TEST:

Give yourself a simple problem. Can't think of one? Don't worry, we've got you covered: get someone to *hide your bag the night before school*. They can't tell you where they've hidden it but they can give you a clue ... the first letter of the hiding place. Don't try to solve the clue now – let your dreaming brain solve it.

Now, as you go off to sleep think about the bag and how much you want to find it. Remember, if you can't find it the next morning you'll get in trouble at school. That should get your anxiety levels up and increase the chances of you dreaming about it.

Based on our tests, if you remember any dreams the next morning there's a decent chance it'll be about finding the schoolbag. And there's a really good chance you'll be correct. Congratulations! You've just dreamed the future.

But even if you don't remember the dream, your sleeping brain probably came up with some brilliant ideas. See how quickly you can find the bag. Anything under a minute suggests your brain has been busy dreaming about the future.

SECRET NUMBER 90

HOW TO RAISE ONE EYEBROW

EVERYBODY THINKS:

You're either born able to raise one eyebrow, or you're not.

BUT SECRET 90 IS THIS:

One in four people are naturally able to raise one eyebrow, but anyone can learn. And it can be really useful.

A raised brow can be used to show agreement, surprise, fear, disbelief or disapproval and to send a silent greeting. It's a secret language all of its own and it can be used to get a confession if you ever become a police officer or secret agent.[48]

PUT IT TO THE TEST:

EYEBROW RAISE STEP-BY-STEP:

STEP 1:

Use your fingers to hold one eyebrow up and the other eyebrow down to get used to the feeling.

STEP 2:

Practise lifting and lowering both brows in front of a mirror without your hands, then try lifting just one.

STEP 3:

Lift your dominant hand eyebrow first. So, if you're right-handed work on your right eyebrow and vice versa.

STEP 4:

Do 30 repetitions every day for two weeks to build up the muscle and you'll have it cracked!

---

[48] See *How to Be a Kid Boss* **Secret 83: How to become a secret agent**.

ECRET NUMBER 91

HOW TO SURVIVE IN SPACE (WITHOUT A SPACESUIT)

EVERYBODY THINKS:

You instantly explode or freeze to death as soon if you go into space without a spacesuit. Lots of movies show this, so it must be true.

BUT SECRET 91 IS THIS:

You can survive in space without a spacesuit, but not for very long. You don't instantly explode or freeze. This is what happens:

YOU WON'T EXPLODE: Oxygen in your body will expand and you'll balloon up to twice your normal size, but you won't explode. Your skin is elastic enough to hold you together. (Top tip: wear stretch pants.)

YOU WON'T FREEZE: for up to 24 hours because heat loss is only though radiation, which is slow. (Top tip: wear shiny underwear to reflect back the heat radiation.)

YOU WILL MAKE A MESS: The vacuum of space will cause gas to expand rapidly, meaning you will poo and wee yourself instantly. And projectile vomit. (Top tip: don't worry about it, better out than in.)

YOUR LUNGS MIGHT EXPLODE: But only if you hold your breath. If you do, the air in your lungs will expand rapidly causing them to explode inside your body. (Top tip: don't hold breath.)

YOU EYEBALLS MIGHT BOIL: But only if you keep them open. Exposed liquid on your body will begin to vaporize. So, the surfaces of your tongue and eyes could boil. (Top tip: keep your eyes and mouth shut.)

PUT IT TO THE TEST?

Please don't.

SECRET NUMBER (92)

HOW TO SURVIVE THE NORTH POLE (WITHOUT A SNOWSUIT)

EVERYBODY THINKS:

You'd freeze to death in about a minute.

BUT SECRET 92 IS THIS:

The Arctic can be surprisingly pleasant in the summer. But we want to know how to survive in a T-shirt and shorts in in winter, when it's -40°C. For that, you need to understand how you'd freeze to death…

HEAT LEAVES YOUR BODY IN THREE WAYS:

1. CONVECTION:
Heat leaves through the air.

2. CONDUCTION:
Heat leaves through objects you touch. Liquids and solids conduct heat much faster than gases such as oxygen.

3. RADIATION:
Heat leaves through infrared waves.

But remember! Your body is generating heat all the time as it turns food into energy. This is called thermogenesis and it creates about 100 joules per second – about a tenth of the energy of an average electric heater. So, all you need to do is make sure you lose less than 100 joules of heat every second. We've worked out how to keep heat loss below 100 joules even on an Arctic winter night, you just need the following:

1. **SHINY T-SHIRT AND SHORTS** To bounce infrared rays back towards your body.
2. **WATERPROOF SHEETS** Top and bottom in case it rains, because water conducts heat quickly.
3. **4 X WINTER DUVETS 60 TOG**[49] Nice and fluffy with plenty of air to slow down conduction.
4. **NO DRAUGHTS** To prevent heat loss through convection.
5. **MATTRESSES** Lots of air to slow conduction
5. **POTTY** Yes, you have to poo in your bed to avoid heat loss.
6. **TORCH** So you can see what you're doing with that potty. (It will also generate another watt of heat energy.)
7. **FOOD** You'll need plenty.

CRET NUMBER 93

HOW TO WAGGLE YOUR EARS

EVERYBODY THINKS:

Ear waggling is even harder than one-eyebrow-raising.

BUT SECRET 93 IS THIS:

Ear waggling is impressive, and anyone can learn to do it. You use 3 ear muscles:

PUT IT TO THE TEST:

STEP 1: Wake up the muscles by darting your eyes from side to side – you should feel your ear muscles working slightly.

STEP 2: Strengthen these muscles by waggling your ears much as you can. Do it 30 times a day for two weeks.

STEP 3: Freak people out by waggling your ears and saying, "I can hear your thoughts!" in a creepy voice.

---

[49] Tog is the unit of duvet warmth. They normally go from one tog (for summer) up to 15 tog (for cold winters).

SECRET NUMBER 94

HOW TO NOT GET JEALOUS

EVERYBODY THINKS:

Life's not fair and being jealous is completely natural. There's always someone who has got more stuff than you. Or worse still, they're luckier, richer, or just plain better than you. Worst of all … sometimes it's your sibling or friend. So, jealousy is inevitable.

WHY JEALOUSY IS INEVITABLE

BUT SECRET 94 IS THIS:

Jealousy can be useful. It can tell you the difference between what you have and what you want. And it can tell you a lot about yourself: what you fear, what makes you anxious or worried and what motivates you.

The other bit to **Secret 94** is that you don't need to *stay* jealous. There's always something you can do about it. Learning how to use and understand your jealousy – and then deal with it, or simply let it go, is a vital life skill. Luckily, we have discovered a Five-Step Jealousy Plan.

PUT IT TO THE TEST:

THE FIVE-STEP JEALOUSY PLAN:

STEP 1: ACCEPT THE EMOTION

It's OK to feel jealous, so don't beat yourself up over it. Write down what you're feeling in a diary, or tell a friend or family member.

STEP 2: TRACE IT BACK TO ITS SOURCE

Often jealousy stems from fears, worries and insecurity. Jealous of a friend's new clothes? Maybe you're worried they are more popular than you or might find different friends.

STEP 3: ASK YOURSELF, "IF GIVEN THE CHANCE, WOULD I SWITCH LIVES WITH THIS PERSON?"

Try, instead, to see them as the human being they are, with their own struggles and stories. That makes it difficult to feel pain over what they have.

STEP 4: PRACTISE GRATITUDE FOR WHAT YOU HAVE

You might not have everything you want. Most of us don't. But you probably have at least some of it: write down a list of things about you and your life that you're grateful for, or glad about.

STEP 5: GET MORE AND AVOID MORE

Sometimes jealousy will help you focus. Jealous because you weren't player of the match when playing a sport? Practise more.[50] And sometimes jealousy can be avoided altogether. Social media is the single biggest source of jealousy. It can create made-up worlds where everyone *looks* like they're having an amazing life. And it's created an epidemic of jealousy. Try to go without – uninstall for a week and see if you feel less jealous.

---

[50] See **Secret 8: How to become the world's greatest footballer**.

SECRET NUMBER 95

HOW TO GRAB A STINGING NETTLE WITH YOUR BARE HANDS

EVERYBODY THINKS:

Stinging nettles are the worst. They are covered in thousands of tiny hairs, each containing a cocktail of chemicals (including formic acid, the stuff in ant venom). When the hairs break off, they pierce your skin like a tiny needle, releasing the venom. So, don't go near stingers, unless you're wearing gloves and carrying a strimmer.

BUT SECRET 95 IS THIS:

You can grab a stinging nettle without it stinging you by avoiding the hairs breaking off and stabbing you. And for that, you just need the right technique.

WARNING! If you accidentally get stung by a nettle, try this brilliant two-step solution:

STEP 1: Remove stuck hairs with sticky tape.
STEP 2: Slap on some baking powder and water to neutralize the acid. Leave it on for about 15 minutes.

PUT IT TO THE TEST?

No thanks!

HOW TO COMMIT THE PERFECT CRIME

EVERYBODY THINKS:

This secret shouldn't be allowed in a book for children.

BUT SECRET 96 IS THIS:

Even though "Everybody" is probably right – this secret got more votes than any other. So, we had to include it. Here are seven ways to commit the perfect crime:

TIP 1: LOOK INCONSPICUOUS

No one pays attention to a plumber. They just assume they're busy doing stuff and should be left alone. This also works for cleaners holding a vacuum, vicars looking worried, kids reading books, and basically anyone in a hi-vis jacket holding a random tool.

TIP 2: REMOVE ALL EVIDENCE

Police believe the toilet was quickly melted down.

TIP 3: WEAR GLOVES

Unless you have no fingerprints...

TIP 4: WEAR A HAT

So the CCTV can't see your face.

TIP 5: LOOK LIKE SOMEONE ELSE

Fake glasses can be convincing. Fake moustaches? Not so much.

TIP 6: IF ANYONE ASKS

Just say "I don't know, I'm just doing what I'm told."

TIP 7: KEEP IT SMALL

Don't steal a £5 million golden toilet.

PUT IT TO THE TEST?

We don't really recommend a life of crime. But please check out **Secret 100: How to break the rules and get away with it**.

SECRET NUMBER 97

HOW TO FIND THE END OF A RAINBOW

EVERYBODY THINKS:

You can't find the end of a rainbow because it's just an optical illusion, and it moves as you run towards it. A rainbow is something to do with rain drops bending different colours of light by different amounts. There's no gold and no leprechauns.

BUT SECRET 97 IS THIS:

You can find the end of a rainbow, but it's not where you think. First, you need to understand what a rainbow is:

1. You only see a rainbow when your back is to the sun and there's rain in front of you.

2. The white sunlight splits into colours inside the raindrops because each colour of light travels at a different speed in water, causing it to change angle

3. The colours of light are then bounced back towards you.

4. Any one raindrop will send one colour of light towards your eyeball depending on its height in the sky and the angle needed to reach you.

5. So, red light will come from higher raindrops and violet light will come from lower raindrops.

A rainbow isn't an arc or a circle, it's actually a cone of colour with the tip right in your eyeball. So, if you want to know where the end of the rainbow is, it's in your eyeball! Sadly, there is no gold – and no leprechauns – there.

If you want to make a rainbow all you need is a shower, a torch and to wait until night-time.

PUT IT TO THE TEST:

MAKING A RAINBOW AT HOME IS EASY.

STEP 1:
Turn on the shower.

STEP 2:
Turn off the lights.

STEP 3:
Turn on the torch.

STEP 4:
Get someone to hold the torch behind and above your head.

SECRET NUMBER 98

HOW TO TALK TO SOMEONE YOU'VE NEVER MET

EVERYBODY THINKS:

Talking to someone you don't know is really hard and scary because it's impossible to know what to talk about and things might go horribly wrong.

BUT SECRET 98 IS THIS:

Talking to someone you've never met gives you "first mover kudos". They will instantly assume you have high social status personality traits like: confidence, openness and intelligence. Here are some top tips for chatting to someone new:

READ THEIR BODY LANGUAGE:

Do they seem open to a conversation? (See **Secret 4: How to tell what someone is *really* thinking.**)

SKIP THE SMALL TALK:

Don't talk about the weather, it's boring.

MAKE EYE CONTACT:

If you struggle with this, use the triangle trick. Look at one eye, then the other, then their mouth.

START WITH AN OPEN QUESTION:

Open questions can't be answered by a simple yes or no.
Try questions like:

PUT IT TO THE TEST:

This is the hard bit. Because it can be scary, especially if you get stuck in an awkward conversation. So have something planned so you know how to wrap it up and move on. It can be as simple as: "OK, I'd better get to..." and then fill in the blank.

> **WARNING!** Not everyone will want to chat, but don't worry and give yourself a pat on the back for trying.

SECRET NUMBER 99

HOW TO READ SOMEONE'S MIND

EVERYBODY THINKS:

Mind-readers, just like fortune-tellers and séances for talking to ghosts, are a huge con. It's just tricks used by stage magicians and at fairgrounds to get gullible people to part with their cash.

It's all just a scam.

BUT SECRET 99 IS THIS:

Scientists can actually now read people's minds just by looking at the pattern of activity in their brain. The bad news is that you need a massive MRI scanner to do it and they cost a fortune (even second-hand they're about £25,000 + postage).

But if your pocket money doesn't stretch to a hospital-grade scanner, don't worry. There's a version that only costs 2p. This is how you do it...

PUT IT TO THE TEST?

THE SHAPE MIND-READING TRICK

STEP 1: ASK SOMEONE TO "THINK OF A SHAPE LIKE A SQUARE, BUT NOT A SQUARE." (Most people think of a *triangle*, especially if you make a subtle triangle shape with your hands.)

STEP 2: ASK THEM TO "THINK OF ANOTHER SHAPE AROUND THE FIRST SHAPE." (Most people will think of a circle because there aren't many shapes that fit neatly round a triangle.)

STEP 3: AMAZE THEM BY DRAWING THIS:

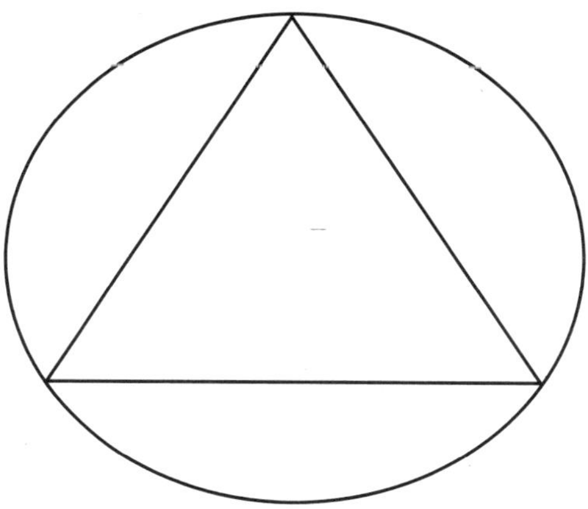

This works because we unconsciously move when we think something (the technical term is ideomotion). It's the same principle behind Ouija boards (see *How to Be a Kid Boss,* **Secret 6: How to be a ghostbuster**).

SECRET NUMBER (100)

HOW TO BREAK THE RULES (AND GET AWAY WITH IT)

EVERYBODY THINKS:

You must follow rules to the letter or you'll be expelled from school and eventually be put in prison. Rules are important, they keep us safe and make sure everyone is treated fairly. And most importantly, they bring order – without rules there'd be chaos.

BUT SECRET 100 IS THIS:

Sometimes it's OK to break the rules. Rules do keep things fair and safe and reduce chaos, but that doesn't mean we should follow all the rules all the time. The greatest people in history broke the rules. Rosa Parks, Nelson Mandela, Florence Nightingale, Galileo, Frida Kahlo, Ada Lovelace (to name a few) changed the history of the world by breaking rules.

But you can't just do it randomly – you'll just get into trouble and annoy everybody. Like it or not, there are some "rules" to breaking the rules. So, before you go full maverick, make sure the situation fits these:

THIS IS WHAT THE WORLD WOULD LOOK LIKE WITHOUT RULES:

THE FOUR RULES TO BREAKING THE RULES

RULE 1: KNOW YOUR VALUES
What's most important to you? Fairness? Success? Having fun? What it two of your values clash? Which one comes out on top?

RULE 2: KNOW WHY YOU'RE DOING IT
Maybe it's for fun, or laughs, or to make you more popular. But always know why you're breaking a rule and if there's an alternative to breaking it.

RULE 3: CALCULATE THE RISK
What are the chances you'll get caught?

RULE 4: BE PREPARED FOR THE CONSEQUENCES
Know what could happen next.

PUT IT TO THE TEST:

Or don't. You don't *have* to break rules if you don't want to. But it's a good idea to at least think about it now and again. Following rules for the sake of it can mean you're trapped into following rules all the time even when it's not for the best. If you want to start small, check out **Secret 32: How to cheat at Monopoly**.

SECRET NUMBER 101

HOW TO READ SOMEONE'S MIND (AGAIN)

EVERYBODY THINKS:

You can just use the Shape Mind-Reading Trick – see **Secret 99: How to read someone's mind**.

BUT SECRET 101 IS THIS:

The Shape Mind-Reading Trick doesn't always work. There's always the odd person who thinks of a dodecahedron. So, double your chances of success with the even easier, Carrot Mind-Reading Trick.

PUT IT TO THE TEST:

THE CARROT MIND-READING TRICK

STEP 1: Using an orange felt-tip pen/pencil, write down the word "carrot" on a piece of paper and fold it over. Give both the pen/pencil and the paper to a friend, but tell them not to look at the paper ... yet. Let them hold on to it so they know there's no cheating going on.

STEP 2: Next, ask them "What's 1+1?" and wait for them to answer. Then ask "What's 2+2?" and wait for them to answer. Keep going until you get to 8+8.

STEP 3: Ask them to name any vegetable.

Nine times out of ten they'll say, "carrot" – and they'll think you're a mind-reader. If you weren't feared for your mind-reading powers before, you will be now.[51]

You might be wondering ... *why bother with all the maths questions?* The maths is just to distract their higher brain functions. When this higher brain function is distracted, our more basic brain goes for the first thing it can think of, and carrots are usually picked because we associate them with orange – the colour of the pencil.

---

[51] If they don't say carrot – you're stuffed. No one will ever respect your mind-reading powers ever again, sorry.

IF YOU'RE FED UP WITH BEING TOLD WHAT TO DO BY EVERYONE, THEN THIS IS THE BOOK FOR YOU!

Discover the secret to brainwashing your parents, making your whoopee cushion smell like a real fart and so much more in this laugh-out-loud guide just for kids.

MORE ABOUT LARRY

Larry Hayes wants to know all the answers to everything. And he wants you to know them, too. Working out of the Secrets Laboratory, Larry has recently learned how to karate chop through a brick wall, predict the future with dreams and make a goat happy just by staring at it. He is also a future Olympic medallist, has never lost a tickle fight and can sleep like a dolphin. Larry's books for children include *How to Be a Kid Boss, How to Survive Without Grown-Ups, How to Survive the Future* and *How to Survive Time Travel.*

ABOUT JOËLLE DREIDEMY

Joëlle Dreidemy has been drawing since she could hold a pencil. Born in Saint-Avold in France, Joëlle went on to gain a diploma from the famous Émile Cohl School in Lyon. She lives and works in Paris, producing illustrations for magazines and children's books.